Jack Flir
Mountain Man

William H. Joiner Jr.

Copyright © 2020 by William H. Joiner Jr.

Published by DS Productions

ISBN: 9798581872154

.

This book is dedicated to my old friend, George Gerald Red Elk. Gerald is a man who sought to keep the Comanche culture, history and traditions alive in the modern world.

Jackson Flint was born in rural Tennessee to Roger and Naomi Flint on January 7, 1848. Roger grinned as he held up his new son. "Jack, my boy, you are a dandy!" Roger handed him back to Naomi who suckled him at her breast as she remarked, "He is a handsome lad." Naomi smiled. "Takes after his pa."

Roger sharecropped cotton on a farm owned by Phineas Cooper. Phineas was known for his ruthlessness with the poor in that part of Tennessee. He scoffed when Roger tried to reason with him about more money. "You got a roof over your heads and cornmeal to eat. What else do you need?"

Roger replied, "Yes, sir. That's sure 'nuff true. We got a shack and cornmeal, but my boy is three now and growing. He needs shoes and a pair of britches once in a while."

Phineas frowned. "Sounds like you're eating too much corn meal. Tighten your belt if your brat needs something else!"

Roger flushed red. "Mr. Cooper, I respect you, but don't call my boy that!"

Phineas responded, "That's the problem with you clod hoppers! You don't know your place. Back when I was a boy, a sharecropper would have never talked like that to my pa. He would have hung 'em up and skinned 'em alive!"

Phineas stared at Roger for a moment before turning to stomp off. Roger grabbed him by the arm. "Mr. Cooper, please, my family needs more than what we're getting. It seems that every year, you charge me just enough to sop up any leftover cash. That ain't right."

Phineas slung Roger's hand off his arm. He angrily shouted, "Are you accusing me of stealing?"

When Phineas wheeled around, he tripped, striking his head on the corner of the steps leading up to the porch of the big house. Blood gushed from the wound. Roger cried out as he tried to stop the bleeding. "Mr. Cooper! Mr. Cooper!" Roger saw the blank look from Phineas' lifeless eyes. He recoiled from the corpse. "Dear God, what should I do? I'm gonna be blamed for this!"

A desperate Roger ran to the barn and quickly saddled up two horses. He galloped back to his shack. Roger shouted, "Naomi, hurry. We got to go!"

Naomi was confused, "Roger, what happened? Aren't those Mr. Cooper's horses?"

Roger continued, "I don't have time to explain it now. Get us a grubstake and grab Jack! He can ride double behind me. Get moving!"

Naomi could see the panic on her husband's face. She lifted Jack behind Roger. Naomi crammed foodstuff in a burlap bag. After mounting the other horse, Naomi followed Roger as they cantered west from the farm.

As they rode, Roger told her of the events that lead to the death of Phineas. Naomi sucked in a breath as she prayed, "Oh, good Lord. Help us!" Roger nervously kept checking his backtrail, expecting to see a posse with a noose bearing down on him. No posse was in pursuit.

What Roger didn't know was every servant who worked for Phineas fled on foot when they discovered his body. Each was convinced that they would be blamed and hanged for the murder of the plantation owner. It was a week before Phineas was discovered. A neighboring farmer noticed the circling buzzards. When the sheriff investigated, he told his deputy,

"There ain't nobody left, but there's a dozen trails leading away. Old Phineas had no family. They all done moved away because he was such a sum bitch! We got more things to do besides traipsing all over Tennessee looking for somebody who probably done the world a favor by killing the old bastard. We'll bury him and that will be that."

Roger and Naomi rode for two days, only stopping long enough to give the horses a breather. Finally, Roger stated, "We can't go on like this. The horses are spent and so are we. I'll try to brush out our trail as best as I can. I'll have to sleep with one eye open." Jack had dozed off and on with his pa holding him on as he rode. Naomi and Jack immediately fell into a deep sleep. Roger attempted to stay awake to watch but nodded off following his family into a sound slumber.

It was dusk when the Flints went to sleep. Roger was awakened the next day by the sounds of the horses grazing. He quickly checked the position of the sun. Roger exclaimed, "Dear God, it's already noon! Naomi, Jack, wake up. We've got to be moving." Naomi stretched as Jack rubbed the sleep from his eyes.

Naomi looked and listened before she spoke. "Roger, honey, did you hear something because I don't see or hear a thing?"

Roger shook his head, "Well… no, but if they catch us, there won't be no trial. They'll hang us on the nearest tree."

Naomi thought for a minute. "Maybe they ain't coming after us. Think about it. Who cares if Phineas Cooper is dead or alive? I don't think anyone would care… If no one cares, why would they come after us?"

Roger's nerves began to settle down. He sighed. "Maybe you're right. Maybe I'm getting all het up over nothing."

For the first time since they fled the farm, Roger began to think about things other than a hangman's noose. He mused, "I reckon we ought to be setting our minds towards where we're going instead of where we been."

Naomi smiled while watching Jack play with a couple of sticks in the leaves. She asked, "Honey, you got any ideas where we could go?"

Roger shrugged. "All I know is folks talk about going west to California. We could try that."

Naomi laughed. "Well, at least that's a plan. We didn't have that five minutes ago."

Roger winked at Naomi as he selected a stone. He was going hunting. When Roger was a boy, he had a reputation among the surrounding farms as a rock thrower. It got to the point that even grown men would challenge him to a rock-throwing contest at various targets. Roger never lost a match. More than one man stalked off muttering, "I ain't seen nothing like it. That boy must have got his arm from God."

Roger didn't need to waste ammunition to add meat to the pot. In minutes he came back carrying a large swamp rabbit by the ears.

Naomi clapped, "Good, I love rabbit!" By rationing the dwindling cornmeal and Roger adding rabbits, squirrels and the occasional possum to the larder, the Flints made it to Ft. Smith, Arkansas.

Roger tied up his horse at the hitching rail in front of Elmer's Livery Stable. As was his habit from years in the horse business, Elmer eyed the two horses from the doorway of the barn. He greeted Roger suspiciously. "That some mighty fine stock you got. Where would you get two animals like that?"

Roger ignored the question. "I'm short of cash. I would trade my horse for a wagon and some boot. You interested?"

Elmer took a closer look, running his hands over the legs of Roger's mare. He straightened up, scratching his head. "We might could work something out... Tell you what. I just took a wagon on a trade. I might could see my way to let you have it and twenty dollars boot."

After examining the wagon, Roger replied as he shook Elmer's hand. "You got a deal."

It didn't take long to transfer their meager possessions to the wagon and hitch up the mare that Naomi had been riding. Elmer spit a quid of tobacco that mostly dribbled down his stained beard. "If you don't mind me asking, where you folks headed?"

Roger grinned. "We're sorta headed to California. All I know about how to get there is to follow the setting sun."

Elmer thought, *How has this pilgrim made it this far?* Instead, he replied, "You'll eventually get there by going west. You need to be careful going through Texas. The Comanche and the Apache are on the prod. The only ones they like killing more than white folks is each other. Watch your hair."

After the wagon began to roll, Naomi was apprehensive. "Roger, I don't like what that man said about the Indians. Maybe we should turn back."

Roger chuckled. "Don't worry about what some old geezer said. Them old men like to tell their stories."

On their way out of Ft. Smith, Roger stopped at a mercantile for flour and bacon. That night the Flints enjoyed a feast of roasted rabbit, cornbread and fried bacon. Roger patted his full belly in front of the roaring fire. He smiled. "Life on the trail might not be so bad after all." It never occurred to him that the large fire would alert anyone who were in the vicinity of their location.

The Comanche and the Apache were always at war. It was their way of life. Life had little meaning without an enemy to kill. The Comanche called themselves *Numunuu* which means The People. The Apache called themselves *Kaisban Dene* which means Our People.

The Comanche Chief was Red Elk. In addition to being a fierce warrior, Red Elk was also a medicine man. In a dream the Great Spirit showed Red Elk a small cactus plant. He told the Comanche, "Eat of the peyote and you will find me." Red Elk's woman was Prairie Flower. Prairie Flower grieved because she was barren. She was ashamed that she bore no children for Red Elk.

The Apache chief was Great Hawk. Great Hawk was the most accomplished fighter among all the Apache. His lodge pole was decorated with many scalps. Most were from Whites and Mexicans, but his most prized scalps were Comanche. Morning Star was Great Hawk's woman. She had birthed two strapping boys, Grey Wolf and Slippery Snake, for her chief.

Their bronze skin glistened in the sunlight as Great Hawk and a small band of warriors watched from hiding as the wagon lurched across the open prairie. Great Hawk's pulse quickened at the impending slaughter of the white-eyes. The Apache chief thrilled at the fear and despair in a victim's eyes when they realized they were doomed at the hands of the Indian. Great Hawk raised his tomahawk as he kicked the ribs of his pony. He burst from the cover of the mesquite thicket, trilling a blood-chilling war whoop.

Roger was paralyzed at the sight of the marauding war party boiling up out of the brush. Naomi screamed as she clutched the toddler to her breast. "Roger, do something!" Roger had briefly considered buying a gun at the mercantile back in Ft. Smith but disregarded the idea as one he couldn't afford. He figured there was no need for a gun with his ability as a rock chunker. Roger instinctively reached for the pile of stones that he had collected, storing them at the front of the wagon. As he started firing the rocks at the attackers, the Apache began to laugh.

A glancing blow from Great Hawk's tomahawk knocked Roger unconscious as he tumbled to the prairie. The Apache preferred captives instead of killing outright when they had a choice. A captive could provide many hours of entertainment. One of the braves ripped Jack from Naomi's arms. As he started to cut the boy's throat with his skinning knife, Great Hawk barked, "No! I want the boy! Morning Star can use his as a slave in our teepee." The rest of the warriors tore off Naomi's clothes, staking her to the ground. When Roger regained consciousness, he was tied to a wagon wheel. The Apache wanted him to have a good view of his woman being ravaged in every way possible that a man could violate a woman.

Roger sobbed, "Leave her alone. She didn't do anything to you."

Great Hawk laughed. "Maybe you could hit us with a rock!"

It wasn't long before Naomi gave up, resigning herself to her fate. Her final words before she died were, "Roger… Jack… I love you."

As horrible as Naomi's death was, Roger didn't realize that his would be much worse. The Apache built a fire on the seated Roger's crotch. As the flames began to burn him, Roger started to shriek. The louder he cried, the louder the Indians laughed. Great Hawk sneered, "The white-eye dies like a woman."

One of the warriors peeled Roger's skin from his body. The Apache felt cheated when they thought Roger died too soon. Yellow Horse was disgusted. "You should cut the throat of his son. How can the boy be anything of value with two women as his parents?"

Great Hawk shrugged. "You may be right, but I will raise him to be an Apache. If I don't like him, I can always kill him. He might make a good slave to sell to the Mexicans or the Comancheros."

Great Hawk arrived at the Apache village with two fresh scalps hanging from his horse's bridle. The entire tribe rejoiced at the return of the successful war party with ear-splitting cries and whoops. Morning Star was especially interested in the young boy riding behind Great Hawk. The chieftain slung Jack down at Morning Star's feet. He commanded, "Make him an Apache!" Morning Star quickly gathered up the boy and hustled him into her teepee. Jack was three years old when he was captured by the Apache.

Great Hawk's two sons were Grey Wolf who was ten and Slippery Snake who was eight. Initially both boys delighted in poking Jack with sharp sticks, hoping to make Jack cry. Morning Star's heart was tender towards Jack. She used her own stick to beat her sons, breaking them from tormenting Jack. She exclaimed, "Leave the boy alone! He is not yours! He is mine! I will be the one to use a stick on him if he needs it!" Great Hawk was chief of the tribe, but Morning Star ruled the teepee.

Great Hawk told her, "Raise the boy in the Apache way. One day I might sell him."

Morning Star responded, "Or maybe I might keep him!" Great Hawk sighed, muttering something that no one could hear.

The rest of the tribe learned to give Jack a wide berth as Morning Star always had her club at the ready. None of the men nor any of the women wanted to challenge Morning Star. More than a few of them carried scars from Morning Star's club. No warrior was fiercer than this woman in a fight. Morning Star named Jack, White Lightning. When Great Hawk saw that Morning Star had named the boy, he despaired at ever selling the boy for a profit. He grudgingly accepted White Lightning as a son.

Grey Wolf whispered to Slippery Snake, "One day we will show that this white boy does not belong as an Apache. I heard the story of how his father died. I'm sure he will turn out like his father, a weepy woman."

Slippery Snake reminded his older brother, "Morning Star is not weepy. She is a woman. Morning Star makes others weep."

Grey Wolf dismissed his younger brother, "Shut up!"

Jack learned to respond to his new name of White Lightning, but he always remembered his old name. Gradually the other children in the village began to include Jack in their games. Great Hawk grunted the first time he put Jack on the back of a horse. "Good. He sits on the horse like an Apache boy." Jack was a natural at horseback riding. This talent earned him the grudging respect of the other Apache.

Encouraged by Jack's ability with a horse, Great Hawk started to teach him the skill of the bow and arrow. By the time Jack was eight, he was the equal of the Apache boys much older than him. One of the Apache boys who was twice Jack's age smirked, "You may can ride a horse and shoot the bow, but that doesn't make you an Apache. No one knows if you can fight because Morning Star protects you. I think you will be like your white father who was a coward." Howling Coyote pushed Jack. "Are you a coward who will run to Morning Star?"

Morning Star watched from a distance. Normally she would intervene, but this time she thought, *It is time for White Lightning to defend himself.*

The crowd of Apache boys grew in number, surrounding Howling Coyote and Jack. Howling Coyote was emboldened when Morning Star didn't come to Jack's rescue. He shoved Jack again, only harder. The bigger boy laughed. "What's it going to be, white-eye? It's beginning to look like you're on your own. Fight or slink crying back to your teepee like a dog!"

Jack noticed that several men and women were now watching the confrontation. Jack wasn't sure why, but he didn't feel any fear. Instead, he picked out a spot on Howling

Coyote's jaw. Jack put his entire body into the unexpected punch. Some would swear afterwards that they heard the crunch of Howling Coyote's jaw breaking. Jack stood over the writhing body of the bigger boy. He said matter-of-factly, "I hear someone crying, but it's not me."

The stunned observers suddenly erupted in the shrill, piercing trilling of the Apache war whoop. The Apache were a great admirer of a fighting spirit. Soon all the men and women were joining in the shouts of an Apache victory. Morning Star laughed at the outcome of the fight, just before she joined in the whoops.

When someone told Great Hawk what had happened, he responded, "White Lightning…? My White Lightning?" Great Hawk bowed up in pride when he verified the report. He announced, "That's my son!" No one looked down on Jack in contempt like before. Even Grey Wolf and Slippery Snake gave Jack respect.

Although, Grey Wolf wasn't completely convinced. He harbored a notion in his mind, *We will see how the white-eye does on his first raid. Only then will we know that he's a true Apache.*

Jack was thrilled in the summer of his tenth year when Great Hawk placed a hand on his shoulder. "I am leading a raiding party in the morning. You will be coming too." Jack noticed that Grey Wolf and Slippery Snake were mounted the next morning as part of the war party.

Scouts had reported that a small band of Cherokees were hunting in Apache territory. Great Hawk and a dozen warriors followed silently behind the two scouts. Every nerve in Jack's body was tingling. Jack didn't know what to expect, but at that moment he knew that nothing was more important than being a warrior.

The Apache watched from a distant ridge as the eight Cherokee braves hunted for the buffalo herd. Great Hawk gave hand signals, dividing and directing his warriors. Jack was in the same group as Great Hawk, Grey Wolf and Slippery Snake.

When they were close enough, Great Hawk trilled the Apache war cry. The rest of the Apache added their voices as the raiders erupted down on the surprised Cherokee. Jack was thrilled. His own war whoop broke into wild laughter.

One Cherokee had not been accounted for. Crow Dancer had lagged behind his Cherokee brothers tending to his lame horse. He ran towards the sounds of battle. Crow Dancer swiftly notched an arrow, sending it into the side of one of the marauder's horses. As his horse fell, Grey Wolf's head struck a rock, knocking him unconscious. The victorious Cherokee grabbed and jerked up Grey Wolf's hair. He screamed the Cherokee war cry as he prepared to scalp Grey Wolf while the Apache was still alive.

Jack had seen Grey Wolf's horse go down, but he didn't realize why until he saw the Cherokee run out of the mesquite thicket. Jack wheeled his pony, charging at the impending scalping. Jack instinctively knew that there was no time to do anything, but to try to run over the Cherokee before he could use his knife. Crow Dancer had started to cut Grey Wolf's scalp when he suddenly saw the screeching Apache barreling down on him. The Cherokee attempted to dodge, but couldn't get out of the way fast enough. The shoulder of Jack's pony struck Crow Dancer, sending him sprawling across the prairie. Jack sprang from his pony without slowing down. He managed to get to the dazed Cherokee as Crow Dancer staggered to his feet. Jack tackled Crow Dancer, slitting his throat before they hit the ground. Jack shrieked in victory as he thrust the Cherokee's bloody scalp towards the sky.

Great Hawk slid his horse to a stop, slipping off its rump and joining Jack in celebrating his first scalp. The Apache chief also realized that Jack had saved Grey Wolf's life. Great Hawk shouted, "I saw Grey Wolf's horse fall, but I couldn't get here in time to help him! Because of you, my son will see the sunrise in the morning." Grey Wolf's respect was the thing that Jack desired most. His heart was full.

Slippery Snake rode up, dismounted and began helping Grey Wolf to his feet. He grinned at his brother. "I saw it all. You owe your life to White Lightning."

When Grey Wolf's head was clear, he grasped Jack's shoulder. Grey Wolf said sheepishly, "I was not convinced that you would make an Apache. Today, I believe. You proved yourself Apache and also my brother." The respect of Grey Wolf was valued by Jack just behind that of their father.

Nine scalps were brought back that day. One of the scalps was from a Cherokee who was still alive. The Apache buried him with just his head sticking from the ground. The defeated brave suffered the humiliation of being urinated on by the men, women and children of the tribe. While the Apache were greatly amused by the degradation of the enemy, they eventually tired of it. Great Hawk coated the Cherokee's head with honey. He spit on him as he remarked, "The Great Spirit has a use for even a Cherokee dog like you. Your head will feed the ants." The Plains Indians had little regards for human life outside of their tribe. The Apache also knew that this would be their fate if captured by a rival tribe.

The Comanche scouts returned to their village reporting to Chief Red Elk. Tall Tree exclaimed, "We have found the Apache. They are camped in a large box canyon with only one way in or out. The canyon has water flowing from the side of a cliff. There is ample grass for their horses."

Red Elk asked, "Can we get in without being seen?"

Tall Tree shrugged. "They have many guards."

Red Elk responded, "I will think on it."

That night Red Elk assembled his most trusted warriors around the campfire. He explained the information that Tall Tree brought.

Ten Bears shouted, "We are Comanche! We will kill the Apache coyotes!" He shrieked his war cry. Ten Bears was joined by the rest of the tribe. The noise was deafening. One did not add his voice to the others.

Red Elk raised his hand for silence. "I will not lead my warriors into certain death for some."

Two days later Red Elk reconvened the warrior council. He announced, "The Great Spirit has given me a plan. For the next week I want warriors, women and children to make many arrows. I want more than we could possibly use for six moons. When we finish, I will lead you to victory over the Apache!" This time Red Elk added his voice to the tribe's war whoops.

Red Elk and his war party left their ponies five miles from the box canyon. They carefully and silently climbed the mountains that lined the canyon. The Apache had several sentries on the rim of the canyon. The Apache had become complacent, feeling that their security was impregnable. The sentries were silenced with a coordinated attack, each bleeding profusely from the knife slash across their throats. In the darkness before the dawn, each Apache sentry was replaced by a Comanche so no alarm would be raised. The Comanche warriors dispersed along the rim as Red Elk had instructed.

As soon as it was light enough to see, Red Elk nodded. The air was filled with whistling arrows. The Apache were surprised at the torrential rain of arrows like a deluge from a thunderstorm. Great Hawk sounded the warning, "Comanche!"

The Apache chief was struck by a half dozen arrows. As he crumpled, Great Hawk muttered, "Great Spirit, why have you let my enemy overtake me?"

Red Elk trilled his war cry at the sight of the dead Apache chief. His voice was swiftly combined with the rest of the warriors.

Disregarding the danger, Grey Wolf covered the body of the Apache chief with his own, crying out, "Father!" Arrow after arrow thumped into the back of Grey Wolf. Blood began to gush from the Apache brave's mouth.

Slippery Snake screamed in despair at the sight of his dead father and brother. In a futile attempt at protecting them, he also covered their bodies with his own, accepting the same fate as theirs.

The Comanche quickly descended on the Apache camp, sparing no one. Every man, woman and child were put to the knife. As Red Elk returned to the Comanche village, he happily thought, *There has never been a greater victory in the history of my people. Thank you, Great Spirit, for delivering my enemy to my bow and knife.*

Ten miles away, Jack was carefully stalking a deer. He grinned as his arrow point pierced the deer's heart. Jack gave thanks for the deer's life. "Thank you, little brother. May your trail in the sky be a good one." After building a small fire, Jack ate his fill of the deer's flesh. He loaded what was left of the deer on the back of his pony. Jack laughed out loud. "I can see the fight between Grey Wolf and Slippery Snake over the rest of this deer!"

Jack became anxious at the large flock of circling buzzards in the direction of his village. The anxiety became a rock in the pit of his stomach as he grew closer. Jack was horrified at the bodies of every Apache that he knew and had grown to love. Jack swallowed hard as he sat heavily in the dirt. He didn't know how long he sat there in a stupor. As he regained focus, anger welled up. "I will take my revenge for my father and my brothers!"

Jack was mystified as the sky darkened. A vision of the Great Spirit appeared. He spoke as a rumble of thunder. "Go, Jack. Vengeance is mine. I have another path for you!" In a split second the darkness was gone. The sky returned to normal. Jack considered everything he had seen that day. He mounted up, pointing his pony west, away from the dead Apache and the live Comanche.

The farther Jack rode, the mountains in the northwest began to draw him to them. He spoke to his pony, Wind in the Sky, "You ever thought about being a mountain horse?

No? Well, get your mind right because you're about to become one."

The voice spoke to him from the darkness of a thicket. "You ain't no Injun like I never seen before. What is you?"

Jack's hand went to the handle of his knife. His eyes strained looking for the man who belonged to the voice. The man nudged his horse out of the shadows. The trapper was dressed in fur with his hat being a wolf's head. He carried a long rifle nonchalantly laying across the front of the saddle. He spoke again, "I asked you a question. What kind of Injun is you?" The language of the man was vaguely familiar to Jack. It had been many years since Jack had heard English.

Jack realized from the question on the trapper's face that he was asking about Jack. Jack pointed to his chest, answering in the Apache language, "I am White Lightning, son of Great Hawk."

The trapper shook his head. "You ain't no Injun." The old man knew enough different Indian dialects that he could piece together what Jack was saying. He continued, "Now that I kinda studied you some, I can tell you're white... You almost had me fooled." The trapper raised his voice. "What's you white name?"

Something snapped in the recesses of Jack's mind. A voice came to him. Jack replied pointing to his chest again. "Jack."

The trapper slapped his thigh and guffawed. "Now we're getting somewhere! My name is Bridger, but I go by Kit." Kit pointed at his own chest. "Kit!"

Jack smiled as he repeated, "Kit."

Kit laughed, "That's right, Jack."

Kit paused before continuing, "Boy, you best throw in with me. I seen lots who came to these mountains and not make it. If the Crow didn't get them, the griz did! Living up high takes some learning. It ain't the same as living down below. 'Sides, I ain't never had no son... at least one that lived. I had a Flathead squaw once. We had a baby. One day I was gone running my traps when the Crow killed them. Cut her throat when they was done with her and bashed little Josh's head in. I tracked them down and killed them for what they done... I never thought much about the boy until he was gone. I miss him something fierce."

On that very first day, Kit spit from his chaw of tobacco. "Jack, we need you to get outfitted with some proper clothes where I won't find your scrawny ass froze to death in some snowbank." Kit led Jack back to his camp. Kit grinned. "Well, here we are. Don't get too attached. We'll be moving on in the next day or two. Can't stay in one place too long before the damn Crow will sniff me out."

Kit pulled out several pelts from a stash of beaver hides. Kit stitched together a shirt and some britches. Jack admired his new clothes. The workmanship equaled the work of the Apache women. Jack smiled and nodded his approval. Kit pointed at Jack's beaded moccasins. "You want new shoes too?" Jack shook his head no. Kit shrugged. "Suit yourself. They might get a little airish." Later Kit added, "I call the lowlanders who try to come up high 'shitheelers.' Most of them have no experience squatting to shit. They aim ain't too good. Get shit on their nice boot heels. Watch out that don't happen to you. Frozen shit on them fancy moccasins might be just the reason a griz would decide that you're the one."

Over the next couple of weeks, the English language came back to Jack. He built on a three-year-old's vocabulary with words that he picked up from Kit, mostly cuss words.

Kit eyed Jack's bow and arrow. "You any good with that bow?"

Jack replied, "I hit what I aim at. I've killed deer and rabbits with it."

Kit snorted, "Out here you got to kill griz and maybe a few Crow. On our next trip to Fort Laramie, I'll trade for a proper Hawken like mine. You're gonna need it in the mountains. These mountains are called the Wind River. It's a great place if you're a trapper like me. I know a valley where the beaver are the size of a buffalo calf!"

Jack laughed. He had already figured out that Kit was prone to exaggeration.

Kit had a small pack mule to tote his hides. He scratched her long ears. "This here is Jenny. I had me a girl down below. Her name was Jenny. This Jenny is a mite prettier than the old Jenny." Kit gave a small shudder at the thought of his old sweetheart.

Buffalo Bob Skinner was the most despised man in the Wind River Mountains. He was also the slickest. Bob specialized in robbing other trappers' string of traps. Kit hated him with a passion after he caught Bob taking a nice fat beaver from one of Kit's traps. Kit didn't ask Bob what he was doing or why. He knew Bob would have a slick lie for cover. Bob didn't know Kit was there until a ball from Kit's Hawken took off most of Bob's ear. Kit shouted after the fleeing thief, "Run, Bob, you mangy dog! Tuck your tail between your legs and run!" Kit complained to his pack mule, "Jenny, how did I miss that skull of Bob's? It's as big as a pumpkin! That sum bitch's luck is going to run out some day."

Before Bob was known as Buffalo Bob, he was known as Capt. Bob. He had used bribery and blackmail to be appointed the captain of a schooner that sailed out of New Orleans. Bob knew little of sailing. He had one purpose in mind. Relying on his first mate, Bob sailed the schooner to a predestined spot where he was welcomed by the notorious pirate, Jean Lafitte. Capt. Bob commanded his men, "Pay no attention to that skull and crossbones flying on their mast. The skipper is a good friend of mine. Lay down your weapons. You will be rewarded richly in a few minutes."

After Lafitte and his pirates boarded the ship, the pirates began tying up the crew members of the schooner. Much to the amusement of Lafitte and Bob, the pirates began forcing the crew to walk the plank. The pirates laughed hysterically as the bound crew members struggled as they slowly sank from sight. Bob's first mate, Lester Greenfield swore, "Damn you, Bob Skinner! One day Davy Jones hisself is gonna rise from his locker and drag your soul to an eternal drowning!" Bob's men began struggling as they saw the fate that was waiting for them. The pirates started shoving the crew overboard in masse.

After the last air bubble from the victims popped to the surface, the pirate chief shook Bob's hand. "You did a good job, Captain. We'll divide the loot and some of my men will sail the schooner to the east coast. I have a buyer in Boston who will pay a pretty penny for a fine ship like this."

Lafitte navigated his ship back to the harbor. That night Bob broke into the hold and stole much more for than his share. He bought a carriage to leave the city, barely escaping the vengeful cutlass of Jean Lafitte. At Shreveport, Bob booked passage on a steamboat to Kansas City.

Bob marveled at the stacks of pelts on the wharf at Kansas City. He asked a passing stranger, "What is all this?"

The stranger smirked, "Where have you been, man? Them's beaver pelts. The American Fur Company is sending them to Europe so the fine folks over there can have the best of hats and coats." It didn't take Bob long for him to calculate that he needed to be in the fur business.

The next day Bob asked the clerk at the office of the American Fur Company, "Where'd all these beaver coats— I mean, pelts—come from?"

The clerk smiled. "They come from all over, but I 'spect most of them come from trappers in the mountains."

Bob added, "What mountains?"

The clerk grinned as he pointed. "West… which is that-a-way!"

Later that day, Bob outfitted himself with a horse, supplies and a mule as he headed towards the setting sun.

Jack bristled at the sight of the two Indians riding toward their camp. He pulled his knife and whispered, "Kit!"

Kit chuckled. "Relax, Jack. Them's two friends of mine. I already knowed they was coming. I been smelling them for a bit. They're Shoshone. Crow smell a bunch different." Kit thrust up his hand in greeting. "Long Hair… Spotted Bear! I seen you boys still got your hair. You done good!"

The two Shoshone silently slipped from their horses. They both stared at Jack. Spotted Bear asked, "Who is this?"

Kit grinned. "You mean ol' Jack? He's sorta like a long-lost son. I'm showing him the ropes on living in these mountains."

Spotted Bear grunted. Long Hair gave a slight nod of acceptance.

Kit motioned to a spot on the ground. "Lite here. I'll get out my pipe. I still got a little tobaccey left." Once the Shoshone and Kit had inhaled the smoke, Kit passed the pipe to Jack. Jack imitated what he saw and took a deep drag. His coughing caused Kit and the Shoshone to break out in laughter. Kit reassured Jack, "You'll get used to it. A good pipe is one of the pleasures in life!"

After Spotted Bear and Long Hair smoked their fill, they mounted their ponies and rode off quietly through the trees. There was no conversation, just a behavior that simplified their life. When Kit and Jack burrowed into their bear skins to join the sun in a night's sleep, Kit murmured, "There's still some things I need to learn you. You need to know about Slew Foot, probably the smartest grizzly that ever lived. You also need to know about Scar. That Crow is the most murderous Injun in these mountains. You'll do good if the bear don't eat you or the Injun don't scalp you. I'll tell you more tomorrow. Right now I'm tired. Smoking always makes me sleepy. Good night."

Jack strained his eyes in the darkness looking for a monstrous grizzly and a killer Indian. It took a bit for him to fall asleep.

The blond grizzly was larger than most females. She had recently bred to Rogue, the largest grizzly in this part of the mountains at fifteen hundred pounds. The female dug for three days building her den. She brought in debris to pad the hole. The weather had turned cold. Her instincts told her hibernation was near. When the den was finished, the grizzly crawled in, circling her bed like a dog before lying down for the winter. The birth of her cub would be the only thing that would wake her up before spring.

After suckling her new cub until her instincts told her it was big enough to leave the den. The female easily broke out with sweeping swipes of her massive paws. The cub eagerly bounded out, experiencing sunshine for the first time.

The grizzly bear is at the top of the food chain. Fear is not a normal emotion to a bear, but fear gripped the momma grizzly as she heard the roar of Rogue. As luck would have it, the mammoth male denned not far from the female. He had emerged from hibernation with a ravenous appetite. The cub looked like a delicious morsel. As Rogue charged the young bear with his cavernous jaws clicking together, the momma bear galloped to intercept the danger to her cub. The female got there, but not before a giant paw from the male sent the cub crashing into the side of a ponderosa pine.

The cub cowered at the furious fight between the two bears. One was driven to protect her cub. The other was driven by his hunger. The growls and rumblings from the combatants echoed and reverberated through the mountains. The female managed to clamp down on the throat of the big male, her fangs glistening with saliva. Rogue used the claws from a hind paw to disembowel the protective mother. Even with her steaming intestines spilling out of her body, the female grizzly tenaciously maintained her grip on Rogue's neck. The ferocious struggle began to lessen as both bears succumbed to the mortal combat.

The blond grizzly died without ever giving up her chokehold on Rogue. Lack of oxygen dimmed the light in the big male's eyes until it was completely extinguished.

The cub mewed and nosed at the carcass of its mother. It began lapping the blood from her body. The oozing blood from their wounds encouraged the young bear to eat the flesh of its mother and father. The cub's back right leg had been dislocated when Rogue had slung the cub against the tree. It never healed properly. The cub went through life with a peculiar ambling gait caused by the turned-out hind leg.

The legend of Slew Foot began that day.

The unmistakable growl of a grizzly jerked Kit from a sound sleep to every cell in his body being alert. Kit could smell the bear. It was close. Real close. Kit slowly closed his hand around the trigger guard of the Hawken, his finger slightly depressing the trigger. Kit always slept with his rifle at the ready. It was primed and ready to shoot. Without moving his head, the old trapper cut his eyes, trying to probe the darkness. A slight movement from the bear betrayed the location of the grizzly. Kit slowly aimed the muzzle in the direction of the threat. When the bear took a tentative step in the direction of the sleeping men, Kit fired the gun where he hoped its head would be. The slug flew true causing the grizzly to squeal as it tossed its head. As the young grizzly thrashed around, Kit wasted no time, rapidly reloading the Hawken.

At the blast of the gun, a shocked Jack sprang from his robe, yelling, "Comanche!" Kit and Jack watched the young grizzly roll in its death throes.

Kit smirked, "You can bet your sweet Aunt Petunia's ass that if that had been Slew Foot, I'd of never heard him. He would be picking his teeth with our bones right about now!" When Kit was sure the bear was dead, he continued, "Well, get that skinner of yourn out. Griz ain't gonna skin hisself."

Jack grinned. "I've skinned deer and buffalo."

Kit replied, "Griz ain't nothing like deer. His hide is thick like a buffalo. Iff'n you do a good job, we'll ride up to Fort Laramie. We'll see how much old man Atkins at the trading post will give for your griz hide."

Scar started out in life as Red Cloud. When he was a young brave, he got into a knife fight with an older Crow. The old man ended the fight with a deep slash across Red Cloud's face. The wound eventually healed, but left a four-inch, jagged scar. Sometimes in the moonlight the white scar seemed to glow. In addition to Scar's nasty temper, the scar unnerved the other members of the tribe. Less than a year later, Scar challenged the same old man to another knife fight. This time Scar cut a gaping hole in his opponent's throat. Scar laughed as he cut the heart from the old man. Scar chewed the heart, slurping the excess blood while the old man was still kicking as he died. Scar changed his name in response from hearing the whispers. He announced, "You no longer need to conceal what you call me. I am no longer Red Cloud. My name is Scar. I will kill anyone who continues to call me Red Cloud!"

Scar watched the four hated Shoshone trespass on what he considered his land. Their ponies glided through the forest effortlessly. The lack of noise was remarkable. The Crow chief was accompanied by only one warrior, River Otter. Scar detested a large war party. Very seldom did his raiding band exceed more than two other braves. Scar thought he was the equal to ten Shoshone. He also hated to share the credit for a successful raid. Scar loved to hear the songs praising his exploits around the evening campfires.

Once there was a promising young warrior who other Crow were beginning to think might be a match for Scar. Scar invited Soaring Eagle on a raid, which was a great honor among the tribe. Scar led the young warrior on a three-day ride to Navajo country. He told the young brave to watch as he butchered three Navajo women who were picking berries far from their village.

Soaring Eagle's forehead wrinkled in disgust. "I don't understand. Where is the honor is killing Navajo women?"

Scar looped an arm around the neck of a surprised Soaring Eagle. The powerful Scar's knife cut Soaring Eagle's throat so deeply that he was almost decapitated.

Back at the Crow camp, Scar told the sad story of being separated from Soaring Eagle and how the young warrior managed to get himself killed by three Navajo women. Scar shook his head slowly as he gravely said, "I was filled with rage that a Crow warrior could get himself killed by women. I took revenge for the Crow nation by killing the Navajo. It only took me a short time. I brought their scalps back to atone for their spilling our blood." Some in the tribe doubted Scar's tale, but no one was brave enough to challenge him on it.

Fort Laramie was a significant 19th-century trading post and military installation in eastern Wyoming. It was located at the convergence of the Laramie and the North Platte rivers. The lowest crossing point for the Rocky Mountains for migrants on the Oregon Trail was nearby. The fur trade was one of the primary reasons for its establishment.

Kit didn't have enough plews or hides to justify a special trip into Fort Laramie. He went anyway because he wanted a rifle for Jack. As they got closer, Kit laughed. He always enjoyed rendezvousing with George Atkins who managed the American Fur Company at the post. The negotiations between the two men were always loud and profane. Most knew that Kit and George were good friends.

Jack turned his head towards Kit. "Well... are you going to tell me what's so funny?"

Kit snickered. "You're about to meet the damndest guy in Wyoming!"

Kit violently threw open the door to the trader's office. He screeched as he saw George, "How in the hell is you still here? I figured some trapper you cheated out of his plews would have bashed your thick skull in by now!"

George bellowed, "I thought I smelled something. I figured that family of skunks is back under the house! I reckon the Crow ain't got ya 'cause they don't want to get close enough to lift your hair!"

Both men strode towards each other, but instead of fighting, they started pounding each other on the back. George finally backed away. "I didn't expect you until it got closer to spring. What happened? The Crow run you off?"

Kit replied, "Hell, no! Every damn Crow in these mountains couldn't run me off! And they know it too!"

George eyeballed Jack, saying, "Boy, I don't know where you come from, but I hope you ain't planning to learn anything from this mangy coyote. Although, you might learn how to skin a poor old trader like me. This old thief robs me blind! When he leaves, I always check to see iff'n I still got my long-handles!"

Kit retorted, "You may be the rudest sum bitch I ever knowed. I been here for five minutes and you ain't offered me a drink yet. Break out the jug, you old skinflint!" Kit nodded toward Jack, "This here is Jack. Jack is sorta my adopted son."

George grinned. "Your son, eh? Boy, did you ever draw the short straw. If you got any sense, you'd skedaddle now before this peckerhead gets you buried up to your hat in a Crow ant bed."

Kit lifted up a Hawken that was propped up in the corner. He narrowed his eyes at George. "How much you want for this smokepole? It don't look like it would even shoot without blowing up. You might could talk me into hauling it off for you. Probably save you a heap of trouble."

George responded, "That's shows how much you know! That's the finest firearm this side of the Mississippi—"

Kit interrupted, "Yeah, yeah… How much!"

George replied, "What you got?"

Kit waved to Jack. "Go bring in your hide." While Jack was gone, Kit continued as he lowered his voice, "George, you take his bearskin straight up for this rifle. Later on, I'll settle up with you on the difference."

George fawned over Jack's bearskin. "This hide is prime… I reckon I could trade my rifle for it… but don't be getting no ideas that I'm throwing in some boot!"

Kit knew the Hawken was worth much more than the skin, but that didn't stop him from carrying on. "No boot? No boot? Don't you ever get tired of skinning folks? I swear, I don't know how you will sleep tonight after cheating this boy like this!"

Jack could see what was going on. "Mr. Atkins, I know you didn't do yourself any favors in this trade, but I'd be proud to own the rifle."

George looked at Kit. "This is a good boy. I sure hope you don't mess him up."

Kit replied, "Shut up and get us some balls and gunpowder. Just showing someone the gun ain't gonna work. We need something to shoot in it!"

Later when they rode away from Fort Laramie, Jack asked, "How much more did you give George?"

Kit spat. "Ain't none of your business if I did... and I ain't saying I did!"

Kit only had to show Jack one time how to load and fire the Hawken. After a few practice shots, Kit gave a low whistle. "Jack, you sure you ain't never shot a rifle before?" Jack smiled as he shook his head. Kit raised both eyebrows. "You may already be as good with that Hawken as I am with mine. You take to that rifle like I take to a hot biscuit."

Kit continued Jack's education regarding how to set traps for beaver. "A big bull beaver is one of the smartest critters alive. If you don't put beaver piss on the trap, you'll never catch one. I keep several sacks of pee that I took from their carcasses. You got to handle it careful-like. If you get any on you, it's the devil to get off! But a bull beaver in his prime can fetch you good money."

Jack and Kit were returning to their temporary camp after a day of laying a new string of traps in a small valley where they had not trapped before. The Crow arrows whistled in the twilight. One arrow grazed Jack's chin before harmlessly thudding into a pine tree. A second arrow broke Wind in the Sky's neck. The old Apache pony was dead before his body hit the ground. Jack was already leaping from his horse when it was struck by the arrow. Jack rolled clutching his Hawken in one hand and his knife in the other.

Kit took two arrows directly in the back. He grunted as he tumbled from his horse. Jack could see that Kit wasn't moving. He knew there was nothing that he could do to help the old trapper until he found and killed the marauding Indians. Jenny squealed as three arrows dug into her side. The pack animal buckled to her knees, before lying gently on her side. Jenny gave a loud snort as she breathed her last.

Jack searched the deepening darkness for the killers. Black Squirrel smirked at the plight of the doomed trappers. He eyed the other two Crow who were part of his raiding party. The old one called Kit had been an ongoing problem for our tribe. Many warriors had set out to kill him. Those who found Kit never returned. Black Squirrel's spirit soared at the thought of the hero's welcome when he returned to the village with Kit's scalp. He smiled at the vision of the braves dancing and singing his praises.

The only thing left to do was to finish the young trapper. Black Squirrel respected Kit. That respect did not extend to Jack. The Crow warrior thought to make short work of the younger man. The Crow were capable of moving swiftly and silently. He nodded to the other two braves. They quietly moved forward to kill the white man.

The thought never occurred to Black Squirrel that this white man was no ordinary white man. Jack may have had white skin, but his upbringing as an Apache made him an Indian. The first Crow never heard or saw Jack until Jack's blade bit into his neck. Jack held him in a vise-like grip until he could noiselessly lay the lifeless body on the carpet of pine needles.

Jack had located the second Indian. He lay motionless as the Crow stepped over him. Jack drove his knife into the brave's exposed groin. The Crow sucked in air as he pitched forward thumping on the forest floor. At that sound Black Squirrel realized that something was terribly wrong. The other two warriors should have already killed and scalped the young trapper.

Black Squirrel strained his eyes, trying to locate the white man. Jack whispered in his ear, "You looking for me?" The Crow shrieked in terror knowing he wasn't dealing with a mortal man, but an evil spirit of the mountains. Jack jumped on the fleeing Indian, bulldogging him to the ground. Jack's blade found the exact spot in the small of Black Squirrel's back that paralyzed the hapless Indian. The light in the Crow's eyes faded until the last twinkle blinked out.

Jack began the grim task of burying Kit. When Jack gingerly turned Kit on his side, Jack's heart jumped with the low moan from his friend. Jack gently lay Kit back on his stomach. Jack knew he was going to have to cut out the arrows. He was afraid that Kit would not survive the removal of the shafts. After building a fire that would cauterize his knife blade, Jack began the delicate task of cutting out the arrows without killing Kit.

An hour later, sweat was dripping from Jack's brow as he laid the second arrow by the first. Jack bound up Kit's wounds with moss from a nearby rock crevice. Jack sighed. "That's all I know to do, Kit... The rest is up to you."

Three days later, Kit regained consciousness. "What are you trying to do? Kill me by starving me to death? Rustle up some grub!"

Jack grinned. He knew if Kit felt well enough to complain, he was going to be all right.

Two days passed until Kit was sitting upright. He asked, "So you're telling me that you killed three Crow warriors all by your lonesome?"

Jack pointed to the three scalps hanging on a tree limb. "You forget I was an Apache warrior."

Kit conceded, "Well... I guess... But you ain't much more than a snot-nose kid."

A week after he had been shot, Kit declared, "We gotta be going. Them Crow you dusted has to have been missed by now. They got braves out searching now. We're lucky they ain't found us already! It's a good thing you were smart enough to hobble their ponies before they high-tailed it back to the village. I'll ride one. You ride the other. The third one will take Jenny's place. I know of some rocky ground that them Injuns can't track us across."

Jack snorted. "I could track you."

Kit retorted, "You can't do no such thing!"

Jack grinned as he nodded. "Even though I was young, I was the best tracker in my tribe. I learned from my father,

Great Hawk. All the Apache said he was the best tracker who ever lived. One day Great Hawk told the village that I had become better than him. He called it a gift from the Great Spirit." Looking at the doubt that showed in Kit's face, Jack suggested, "Why don't we have a test? I will give you an hour's head start. You go across your 'untrackable' ground. I will come and find you."

Kit shrugged. "Okay, but I know I'm going to have to come back looking for you."

Kit rode two miles up a rocky creek before exiting on a bed of loose shale. He chuckled out loud. "Okay, young Jack, unless you can smell like a wolf, good luck on sniffing me out!" Kit continued up a steep climb to the top of a box canyon. He marveled as he patted his horse, "I got to admit them Crow know horses. You're a good 'un." Kit tied off his pony and tore off a plug of tobacco. He savored the taste with a sigh. "When I get my fill of this here tobaccey, I reckon I'll start back to find my lost boy."

Mountain men learn to grab rest when they can. Kit momentarily closed his eyelids. The sixth sense that helped keep Kit alive all these years, alerting him to Indians and predators trying to kill him, sent a warning spiking through his brain. He searched with his eyes, never moving his head. Slowly Kit tilted his head downward locating the sound that disrupted his rest. Kit grinned as he saw Jack picking his way up the steep slope, riding one Indian pony while pulling the other. He spat, "Well, I'll be a suck-egg mule! That boy done it!"

Kit never acknowledged him as Jack slid off the horse. Finally, Kit looked at Jack. "Took you long enough. I figured you'd been scalped or et by a bear by now… You know it ain't easy looking through bear shit trying to figure if a man was in there someplace!"

Jack smiled. "That'll be the day."

Slew Foot's nose wrinkled at the smell of the yearling mule deer. The grizzly remained motionless as the young doe cautiously fed than jerked her head up to check her surroundings. When she got close enough, Slew Foot roared as he charged. The panicked muley slipped on the forest leaves as she frantically tried to escape. When she regained her footing, it was too late. Slew Foot snapped her neck with a jolt from a massive paw. The deer lay bleating as she lay helpless. Slew Foot sank his muzzle in the soft belly of the doe. He ripped out her stomach, intestines and heart with one bite. The grizzly licked his bloody lips as he attacked the steaming insides of the deer. Slew Foot clacked his jaws together as he enjoyed the savory flesh.

At the roar of Slew Foot, all the creatures of the forest and mountains went silent. The big bear was the most feared of any animal in the Wind River mountain range. At times, a grizzly will bury his kill to come back at a later date to finish it. That was not necessary with the yearling. The hungry bear devoured the deer, including grinding up and eating her bones. In the end, the muley's skull was all that remained.

Long Hair and Spotted Bear were two of the bravest warriors in the Shoshone tribe. They had proven their courage in many skirmishes with the Crow. They both had several grizzly bear kills to their credit. While they would be reluctant admit it, deep in the recesses of their minds was an embedded fear of Slew Foot. One night over a small campfire, both Indians jumped at the crack of a nearby branch breaking.

As they sheepishly looked at each other, Spotted Bear laughed. "Slew Foot?"

Long Hair returned the grin. "Yes... That grizzly is not a normal bear. I think he might be an evil spirit born in these mountains."

Spotted Bear nodded. "I have thought the same thing." After listening intently for several minutes and not hearing anything else, the Shoshone were certain that whatever broke that branch was not Slew Foot.

Slew Foot's deep-set eyes cast a tiny reflection from the dying blaze. He controlled his breathing the same as stalking any prey. The night sky was cloudy. There was no light from the stars or moon. From the inky blackness, Slew Foot bolted with a ground shaking bellow. Longhair managed to roll free of the initial charge. A stunned Spotted Bear was pinned to the ground as the passive grizzly disemboweled the Indian with a rip of a rear paw.

Longhair fled screaming, "Aaayyiiii!" His panic increased as Longhair heard the bear chasing him. Longhair continued to shriek. The Shoshone was bowled over by a swat of Slew Foot's front paw. The monstrous grizzly easily held down Spotted Bear as he tore chunks from the Indian's back. When Slew Foot had gulped most of Spotted Bear's flesh, he dragged the carcass back to where Longhair was still alive. The hapless brave was whimpering as he stared at the steam rising from the pile of his intestines laying next to his face. Slew Foot nosed through the guts before swallowing the choice pieces first.

Slew Foot sat on his haunches as he leisurely consumed the rest of the remains of Longhair and Spotted Bear. Occasionally, he would roar a challenge to anything that would dispute his claim as the monarch of the mountains. When Slew Foot finished feeding, the only thing left were two Shoshone skulls.

Far in the distance, Buffalo Bob heard the echo of Slew Foot's roar. Some might have mistaken it as the rumble of distant thunder. Bob shivered in terror at the recognition of what could only be the voice of Slew Foot. The renegade trapper had heard all the stories of Slew Foot when he drank at the bar at Fort Laramie. At first, Bob discounted the tales of the grizzly. "Come on, now. No bear could be that big and that smart!"

The trapper telling the story replied, "You ever seen 'ol Slew? Well, I have! I seen him crossing a valley when I was sitting on a ridge. I liked to have killed my horse getting out of there! Truth is that horse was never the same after that. I rode him so far and so fast, it broke his wind!" Several other trappers chimed in with horror stories about the legendary grizzly.

Bob waited until Tad Gilly had run his trapline, skinned the beavers and set out for Fort Laramie to sell the prime pelts. Tad had only been in the mountains for less than a year, but he was a quick learner. He left his sweetheart back in Tennessee with a promise. "Mary Beth, I want to marry you more than anything else in this world. I just can't do that without enough money to support you. There's nothing for me in Tennessee, but I hear a man who's willing to work can make a fortune in the mountains trapping beaver. I've got to go. I'll be back as soon as I have a poke that will finance a marriage."

Mary Beth sobbed, "Please don't go, Tad. I don't care about the money. As long as we're together, that's all that matters! Indians or bears might get you in those mountains. Please stay!"

Tad gently pried her arms from around his neck. He whispered, "Honey, I've got to try. I wouldn't be much of a man if I didn't."

Bob laid an ambush at a bend in the trail. When Tad and his packhorse came into view, Bob pulled the trigger on the muzzleloader. The ball struck Tad higher on the chest than Bob wanted. The force of the gunshot spun Tad around. He lay face down on the ground. Bob carefully approached his victim. When he was convinced that the trapper was dead, Bob grabbed the sleeve of his coat to turn him over. Tad slashed backwards with the concealed knife. The blade sliced Bob's cheek exposing the bone. Bob swore, "Sum bitch!"

Bob began clubbing Tad with the stock of his gun. With each blow, Tad's head began to shred. His lifeblood poured out, staining the ground red. Tad's last words were a whispered, "Mary Beth."

Bob gasped for air after the lethal beating. "I'll say one thing for you, ol' son. You was hard to kill." Bob laughed out loud when he opened Bob's pouch that contained gold and silver coins. He spoke to Tad's body. "Dammit, I kilt you too soon! No telling how much money you would have had in a couple more months… But you just can't tell about you damn trappers. Some of you might have a good poke. The others drink up everything they make." Bob tightened the strings on the pouch. He continued, "Now, me… I like me a snort of whiskey from time to time… I also like that little Indian whore at the Fort. I'll pay for her too."

Bob sat down on a tree stump after pulling a bottle of rotgut from his saddle bags. He drained it. With a loud burp, Bob sighed. "Well, I guess I'll get to burying you, ol' son. Can't have no one tying your body to me."

Bob looked expectantly at George Atkins. George examined the beaver pelts before looking suspiciously at Bob. "Here's what I don't understand. This is the fourth time you've brought me furs. Each trapper has their own peculiar way to skin a beaver. It's almost like a signature. Every one of your loads look like they were skinned by a different man... Can you explain that?"

Bob shrugged. "Do you want them or not? You ain't the only fur buyer in Laramie!"

George thought for a moment. He stated, "I guess I can't balk at a suspicion. Let me go get the gold out of the safe to pay you."

Scar and his warriors regularly watched what the white man called The Oregon Trail. The wagon trains were usually of sufficient size to contain enough guns manned by the farmers and ranchers to protect themselves. Occasionally, there was an exception.

Lucas Botek, his wife Leeann, their eight-year-old son, Jonah, and their four-year-old daughter, Ruth, were headed west. Lucas had announced over a cornbread supper in their shack in Mississippi, "I think we should move. I know we have some family here. Our family needs a fresh start. Everyone is saying that there are real opportunities out West. I want to pack up and join a wagon train..." Lucas waited for his family to respond.

Leeann replied, "I don't know, dear. I know we've talked about this some, but to actually do it… I don't know."

Jonah jumped right in the conversation, "Yeah, Pa! Let's do it! I want to be a cowboy!"

Ruth went back to playing with her ragdoll.

Over the next couple of weeks, Leeann came around to the urgings of her husband and son. "Well… I'm still not completely convinced. Lucas, if you feel sure about this, let's go West, but only under one condition. If I don't like it, you'll bring me back to Mississippi."

Lucas embraced Leeann tightly. He softly said, "If you don't like it, I'll bring you back."

Jonah pulled on his ma's skirt as he erupted in a raucous celebration. Ruth threw her doll in the air as she joined in the festivities.

Lucas and Leeann had saved up a modest amount of money. They used it to renovate a wagon that had been abandoned on a neighboring property. Leeann's side of the family had died in an outbreak of cholera. Lucas still had his ma and pa. He asked his parents to accompany them. "There's nothing holding you here. Come go with us."

His ma responded, "And do what? Son, we're too old to go on a trip like that. Besides, Mississippi is my home. I was born here. I reckon I'll die here."

Lucas's pa gave a shrug that said, "What can I do?"

Later Ruth asked, "Why was grandma crying?"

Tears began rolling down Leeann's face as she hugged her daughter. "Sometimes grownups cry over grownup things. You'll understand when you get older."

The morning that Lucas, Leeann and the kids were scheduled to pull out, Lucas's pa came by in the predawn. He pressed a small sack into Lucas' hand. "Your ma and me want you to have this. We want to make sure our grandchildren are taken care of." Afterward Lucas looked in the sack to find enough money to finance the trip West.

Lucas picked up the wagon train at St. Louis, Missouri. The wagonmaster held out the agreement for Lucas to sign.

Ward Bond cleared his throat before announcing, "I want to make sure you folks understand and agree with a couple of things. First, as the wagonmaster, I have the final say on anything that has to do with the wagon train. Second, if you decide to turn back at any time, you will be going alone. Once the wagons start west, we don't stop 'til we get to Oregon."

Leeann's face reddened as she nodded to Lucas to sign. She knew her husband was thinking about his promise to bring her back if she wanted.

The trip was fairly uneventful except for a death from a rattlesnake bite and a few of the older folks passing away. The bulk of the trip was behind them as the wagon train entered the mountains of the Northwest.

Lucas had been nursing a wobbly wheel when it finally broke into several pieces. Ward noticed the wagon pulling out of line. He galloped up and asked, "Lucas, you want me to get you some help with that wheel?"

Lucas shook his head. "Nope, I got a new one in the wagon. I can change it out. I don't want someone to have to stop to help me when it ain't needed."

Ward responded, "Suit yourself." He wheeled his horse around, hurrying to get back to the front of the train.

Lucas wrestled the new wheel out of the wagon as Jonah tried to assist his pa. Lucas had a lever and a fulcrum that he had brought along to help change out a wheel. Lucas smiled at Leeann. "See, I got everything we need. A man's got to be able to rely on himself."

As the last wagon disappeared from sight, Leeann became nervous. "Honey, I wish you'd hurry. I don't like not being able to see the other wagons."

Lucas grunted. "There must be some kind of burr on the axel. This wheel should have slid right on. Something's putting it in a bind... I'll take it off and see if I can figure out the problem." Leeann kept glancing in the direction of the trail made by the wagons. Lucas said soothingly, "Don't worry. We'll catch up in no time."

Lucas and Leeann assumed they were alone. That changed when an arrow thudded into Lucas' neck. The point of the arrow was on one side, the fletching on the other. Lucas made strangling noises as he sank to his knees clutching his throat. When he toppled over on the prairie grass, the shock for Leeann set in. She began to scream hysterically. Jonah and Ruth joined their mother in shrieking at the sight of their dying husband and father.

Scar jerked his arrow from the white-eye's neck. He screamed the Crow war cry as he lifted Lucas' hair, slicing his scalp from his skull. The other three Crow warriors were busy tearing the woman's clothes from her body. Scar didn't join in the abuse of Leeann. He preferred killing over sex. Finally, he pushed his braves away. "We have other things to do. You will be back to your squaws soon." Scar stuck the point of his knife in the bottom of Leeann's belly. He ripped the blade upward, laying bare her internal organs. Scar ordered his warriors, "Take the children back to our village. They can help the women." Scar proudly tied the scalps of Lucas and Leeann Botek to the bridle of his war pony.

Ruth lived for two days after being brought back to the Crow village. She had slipped into a catatonic state. One of the Crow women had enough. "What good is this girl? She hears nothing. She sees nothing. She does nothing! Our warriors need to bring those who are useful!" The squaw caved in Ruth's head with a blow from a knobbed club.

Jonah lasted a week. With all his family killed before his eyes, Jonah managed to work free of his bindings late one night in a desperate attempt to escape. Scar easily caught up to him the next day, sending an arrow into his back. There were no known answers of what had happened to the Botek family outside of the Crow village. That memory quickly faded as the Crows went about their everyday business.

Kit spit a quid on the ground exclaiming, "I been holding that for a while. I had to wait until we was done resetting our traps. Ain't nothing says 'man' like tobaccey juice to a big bull beaver. I've watched them dive back in the water at the first whiff of tobaccey. Then they would slap the water with them flat tails. They was telling me, 'We know you're out there!' You done good not taking up the habit."

Jack's nose wrinkled. "I ain't never understood why a man would chew something that should be smoked."

One day Jack and Kit split up to run separate traplines. Jack caught his breath when he saw the cow elk grazing along a game trail up the mountainside. Jack slipped off his horse, using the saddle as a rest as he sighted the Hawken on his target. Jack murmured softly, "I can taste those elk steaks now. Ain't nothing better." Jack pulled the trigger. The ball popped the hide of the elk, creating a small puff of dust. The bullet passed through the heart. The elk dropped in its tracks. It never knew what hit it.

Jack was usually thoughtful about his actions. Today in his haste to get to the elk, he made a mistake. He forgot to reload his rifle.

The pack of eight wolves were hungry. They had been tracking this elk for the better part of an hour. The rifle blast caused them to crouch. Their leader snarled at the prospect of his meal disappearing. He watched the hated man leading his horse approaching the fallen elk.

When Jack got closer to the carcass, he saw a shadowy figure slink between two pine trees. Jack froze looking for further movement. His pony wrinkled its nose, smelling something it didn't like. The horse began to nervously shift its feet at first, then started pawing the ground. Jack could count three wolves, but suspected there were more. He tried to calm the horse, "Easy now. Wolves ain't that big a deal. We can handle them."

The horse reared and squealed when the large black wolf stepped out of the dense cover. The wolf pack leader was driven by hunger to take a risk he normally would not have taken. The hackles on his neck bristled as he snarled a warning. Saliva dripped from his fangs. When he emerged, the other seven wolves showed themselves with threatening growls.

Jack was struggling to keep control of his pony. The horse mule-kicked, pulling the reins out of Jack's hands. Jack dove at his mount. He managed to pull the Hawken from its scabbard before his horse galloped away. The problem was his gunpowder and musket balls were in the saddlebags of the panicked pony.

With his unloaded rifle in one hand and his skinning knife in the other, Jack began to back away from the wolf pack. He said softly, "Okay, I get it. You want the elk... No problem, you can have it... If I can catch that damn horse, I might let you have it too." Instead of being content with the cow elk, the wolves sensed they had the advantage. They continued toward Jack.

One of the wolves had silently slipped around behind Jack, a familiar move when cornering a prey animal. Jack never saw the wolf, but the gaunt gray wolf made its presence known when it leaped upon Jack's back, knocking him down. Jack twisted on the way down, narrowly avoiding a vicious snap of the wolf's jaws. Jack knew he was in a desperate situation. He reverted back to his basic instincts as he snarled and slashed at the attacking wolf. The blade ripped open a large gash in the wolf's belly. It yipped in pain.

Jack managed to regain his feet as two more of the marauders sank their teeth in an arm and a leg. Jack used his free arm to swing the Hawken like a club. The skull of one of the wolves was crushed, forcing it to release its grip on the other arm. The third wolf was shaking Jack's leg like a dog shaking a rat. Jack drove his knife in the back of its neck. While its blood seeped out of the wound, Jack snarled and howled at the rest of the pack. For the first time since the attack began, the rest of the wolves hesitated. They started to back off. Jack bared his teeth and continued to growl.

That night when Jack's horse trotted into camp, Kit quickly snatched the reins. He demanded, "Damn you! Where's Jack?" Kit couldn't find any blood on the saddle or the horse, but he knew that the search for his partner couldn't wait until morning. Kit grabbed his own horse and began backtracking Jack's horse by the light from the stars.

To make a bad situation worse, a light snow began to fall threatening to cover the hoof prints. Kit swore as he trudged ahead looking for Jack. The snow on the trail up ahead moved. A low moan came from the fresh snow. Kit hurried and wiped aside the snow. Kit breathed a sigh of relief. He muttered, "Jack, my boy, what are you doing there?" When Kit uncovered his partner, he could see the bite wounds in Jack's arm and leg. Fortunately, the cold had slowed down the blood loss. Kit tenderly draped Jack over his horse. On the way back to camp, Kit exclaimed, "Don't you ever pull this shit again, Jack. You've taken some years off my life… I ain't got that many to spare!"

Jack was recovering from his wounds thanks to some herbal treatment that Kit had learned from the Shoshone. In a couple of days, Kit went to retrieve the pelts from the three wolves Jack had killed. There wasn't much left of the wolves or the elk. The surviving ravenous wolves had devoured the meat and most of the hides. The only things left were skulls and a few bones. The sight of the remains made Kit quickly scan the area. The thought of wolves that hungry was a little spooky to Kit.

Casper Fortenberry arrived at Fort Laramie in style. Instead of traditional Western or mountain garb, Casper was decked out in a suit, spats and a stylish derby hat. A thick, tailored beaver coat kept the dandy warm. He was accompanied by his butler, Cheeves. Rip Thornton was an experienced mountain man. He had agreed to guide Casper when the marshal in Kansas City who was a childhood friend of Rip's told him about a greenhorn with money who was looking for a guide to Fort Laramie.

When the traveling party arrived in Laramie, Rip went directly to the saloon. He told the barkeep, "Two bottles of whiskey. As soon as one runs out, get me another bottle. I want to make sure I got plenty!"

The bartender grinned. "I ain't seen you in quite a while. Have a rough trip from back East?"

Rip gulped another shot of rotgut. "You ain't got no idee, Fred, what I been through. Now shut up and let me drink!"

Casper, with Cheeves in tow, pushed open the office door to the American Fur Company. He strode over to George Atkins who was sitting behind his desk. Casper thrust out his hand. "You must be George Atkins. I've heard some excellent things about you. You're going to be my new office manager."

George's jaw dropped as he shook Casper's hand. "Wh... what?"

Casper adjusted his tie. "The American Fur Company has had its day in the sun, but New York Skins is putting the old girl out of business."

George scratched his head. "I don't know nothing about American Fur shutting down... Who are you with now?"

Casper walked around the office as if evaluating everything. Cheeves stood dutifully in the corner. Casper wheeled around to George. "New York Skins, man! If you want to work for me, you're going to have to pay attention!"

George sputtered, "I ain't going to work for you! I don't even know you... Say, did ol' Kit put you up to this? Where is he? I bet he's waiting outside ready to bust in here laughing his fool head off!" George marched to the door, sticking his head out, "Kit, damn you! I got more to do then messing with you!"

When he didn't get an answer, George walked back to his desk in confusion. Casper looked at Cheeves. "These frontier persons are a little strange." Cheeves slightly raised an eyebrow in acknowledgement. Casper addressed George. "Maybe I didn't make myself clear. I own New York Skins. My company is taking over the fur trade in Fort Laramie. You can either go to work for me or you can swamp at the local drinking establishment. I can assure you my offer is more lucrative."

George studied Casper then asked, "And you're sure Kit Bridger don't have nothing to do with this?"

Casper retorted, "I don't know this Mr. Bridger. I'm trying to offer you an opportunity to make money. If you insist on being preoccupied with this Kit fellow, I may focus my attention elsewhere."

After Casper left the office, George couldn't resist looking outside one more time for any sign of Kit.

No one except Casper knew that Cheeves was not who he appeared to be. His name wasn't even Cheeves. That was the name assigned to him by Casper when he was hired.

Cheeves' real name was Archibald Smythe. At one time Smythe was head of the constable force in London. Smythe used his position to run a crime ring. His syndicate came unraveled when a couple of his henchmen killed a member of the Royal Family during a holdup. Smythe barely escaped the chopping block, catching a schooner headed to New York.

Casper was drinking at a pub in New York City when he was approached by Smythe. Smythe extended his hand in introduction. "Good evening, sir. I have come to understand that you're always looking for a good man for your enterprises. I think I understand the nature of your business. You could use a chap with my... skills." Casper refused his hand. It appeared to be unwashed. Smythe continued, "If I may, I am experienced in the things that you might find useful. I was head of the police force in London, England, but my real business was robbery, extortion and murder for hire. I also have a thorough understanding for the need for discretion." Casper's countenance changed for one of indifference to one of interest.

Casper responded, "Sit down, Mr. Smythe. Perhaps we can do some business." After a few more glasses of ale, Casper leaned forward and whispered, "I am selling my businesses here. I plan to take on the American Fur Company. I want to capture the rights to buy and sell fur for the entire United States. Maybe you could be the right man to accompany me on a trip to the Northwest. My businesses here are two bits compared to the huge amounts available trading in beaver pelts. I need a man who can handle a sticky situation without becoming squeamish. I have no use for a woman, except for the obvious."

Smythe cut in. "Say no more, Mr. Fortenberry. There is no task you can give me that I can't handle."

Casper strummed his fingers on the table as he studied Smythe. He replied, "I like your can-do attitude. I don't deal in excuses. If you're the right man, you will become wealthy. If you're not... well..."

Casper had rented two adjoining rooms at the boarding house in Fort Laramie. Even though Mrs. Olsen said it was highly unusual, Casper paid her enough money to have breakfast for him and Smythe brought to his room every morning.

Smythe asked, "What's next, boss?"

Casper retorted, "The first thing is to eliminate the competition, but all in good time. I don't want to make a move until we have been here for a couple of weeks."

Two weeks later, George was headed for his bungalow at the edge of town. The rifle blast shook the peace from Fort Laramie. The ball struck George squarely in the middle of the back. It exited at his sternum, creating a hole that one could see his spine. George flopped on the ground. His eyes stared unseeingly at the footing of the house.

George Atkins was extremely popular with the citizens and the military of Fort Laramie. Folks were clamoring for something to be done. The office of Major Henderson was jammed with shouting people. He motioned for quiet. "Settle down. You're making so much noise I can't hear myself think!"

The local blacksmith, Angus Blackburn, yelled, "Major, what are you going to do? We can't have decent men like

George Atkins murdered on our streets!" The din of the crowd increased.

Major Henderson commanded, "Shut up! Shut up or I'll have my men clear this room!" The four soldiers standing at ease in the back of the room didn't look thrilled about dispersing the angry mob. The major continued, "I'm just as upset as you. George Atkins was also a friend of mine. We will find the killer, but I'm going to need some time to conduct an investigation. Now clear out so I can get to work!"

The blacksmith muttered to a man next to him as they exited the office, "Just what I figured. Total bull squirt!"

The word got out about George's funeral. Mountain men came in numbers usually reserved for rendezvous. Bigfoot Fincher thundered at Kit and Jack as they were resetting a trapline deep in a valley, "There you are! I been looking high and low for you." Kit and Jack craned their necks looking up on the mountain ridge.

Kit was exasperated, "You durn fool! Pipe down before you scare away every beaver in this part of the Wind River!"

Bigfoot shouted back, "It's George! George Atkins is dead!"

Jack was stunned. "We just saw George not too long ago. He looked like he could live to be a hundred."

Kit scratched his beard. "Bigfoot has been known to tell some windies, but we better get up there to see what he's caterwauling about." When Kit got close enough to see Bigfoot's face, a knot formed in his gut. Usually Bigfoot told his biggest windies when he was knee-walking drunk. Bigfoot's drunks were accompanied by a bright red face. Kit could see that Bigfoot's face was pale, like all the blood had drained out of it.

As soon as Kit and Jack were close enough to carry on a conversation, Bigfoot began. "It's true. George is dead. Some polecat bushwhacked him. Shot him in the back! Some damn coward!"

Kit demanded, "Who done it?"

Bigfoot responded, "Ain't nobody knows. That damn major is supposed to be conducting some kind of invest-ti-gation. I don't think that boy could find his ass with either hand if somebody held his hat."

Kit paused for a moment before grimly answering, "I'll find out."

Jack had never seen Kit act like this. He would have expected his partner to cuss up a blue streak. Kit clammed up and wouldn't speak unless spoken to.

Major Henderson jumped as it sounded like someone had kicked his door off its hinges. The reason it sounded like it was because someone did. Kit stood in the doorway with the shattered door at his feet. Kit asked softly, "Have you found him yet?"

The major exclaimed, "That door was government property! You can't just go around destroying government property! Somebody's got to pay for that!"

Kit raised his voice slightly. "I ain't gonna ask you again. Have you found George's killer?"

Henderson waved away the soldiers with weapons at the ready who charged in. "I got it." The major stuttered, "I-it..

It's complicated, Kit… But I got some of my best men working on it. I 'spect we'll have some good leads anytime now."

Kit snorted in disgust. When he wheeled around to leave, he almost bumped into Jack. Jack had been hurrying to catch up with his partner. Jack didn't want a war with the army. Kit brushed by him. "Let's go. I swear I'll find the man who done this to George!"

Kit began asking questions. He started with Bigfoot. "Anybody had a beef with George lately?"

Bigfoot shook his head. "You know as well as I do that everybody liked George. Even when he got the best of you in a trade, you almost felt like thanking him for it."

Kit laughed for the first time since he heard about George's death. "Yep, that was George all right. Damn, I'm gonna miss that sum bitch." Jack felt better hearing Kit cuss.

Jack grinned. "That ol' George was a real sum bitch!" Kit laughed harder.

Kit began hearing about the new fur buyer in Laramie over the next couple of weeks. He was approached by Casper. Kit heard the buyer was strange, but he wasn't prepared for the figure in a suit and bowler hat.

Casper smiled. "You must be the famous Kit Bridger I've heard so much about!" Casper extended his hand. As Kit gradually shook it, Casper continued, "It's a real pleasure, sir!" Casper turned. "This is my associate, Cheeves."

Kit nodded at Cheeves as the hair stood up on Kit's neck. Kit made a mental note to always keep track of Casper's servant.

Kit motioned towards Jack, saying sarcastically, "And this is my associate, Jack Flint." Casper extended his hand towards Jack. Jack's response was a little frostier than Kit's. Jack refused to shake.

Casper pretended not to notice. Casper smiled again. "I just want you gentlemen to know that my company, New York Skins, is paying top prices for pelts. With the unfortunate passing of Mr. Atkins, I felt compelled to be of assistance to the trappers. I expect that the American Fur Company will eventually replace Mr. Akins, but it may be months before they are back in business."

Kit replied, "I'll keep that in mind."

When they were alone again, Kit asked Jack, "Well, what did you think? I seen you be a mite more friendly."

Jack responded, "What do I think? I think you just shook hands with the man who killed George."

Kit furrowed his brow. "Now how the hell did you come up with that? You don't know anything about the man and you only seen him for five minutes!"

Jack shrugged. "I know what I know. Great Hawk taught me to trust my gut feelings. He said it was the Great Spirit giving truth to those who would listen."

Kit grunted. "Maybe."

Jack added, "And that ain't all. The associate, Cheeves, is a dangerous man. It wouldn't surprise me at all if he was the one who pulled the trigger on George. He has a killer's eyes."

Kit nodded. "The hair on the back of my neck got the same message."

Kit and Jack carefully examined the location where George was shot. Jack pointed at the ground. "See those little scratch marks? Someone has brushed away the tracks. This wasn't no spur of the moment killing. It was well thought out."

Kit asked, "You still think it was that Casper feller and his boy?"

Jack answered, "Who stood to profit with George out of the way?"

Kit's blood began to boil. "Why, that bushwhacking coward! I'm going to give him what he gave George!"

Jack grabbed Kit's shoulder to restrain him. "Now hold on! You can't just gun him in the middle of town. That would get you crossways with the army! We need to find some evidence to file a charge. Let's be smart about this."

Kit sighed. "Okay, we'll try it your way... but one way or the other, them sum bitches are gonna pay for what they done to George!"

Casper had rented a building down the street from the American Fur Company. The owner of the building tried to sell Casper the building or get a long-term lease. Casper shook his head. "That's a fine offer, but I think I'll wait to see if the American Fur Company does indeed reopen. Their building might become available. Stranger things have happened."

Dealing with Casper left a lump in Bigfoot's throat. He had to fight a gagging reflex, but Bigfoot felt like he had no choice. The trapper was out of money. Bigfoot offered guardedly, "I can hold on to my prime pelts if I want to, but I thought I'd give you a shot at buying them."

Casper grinned. "Let's have a look." After going outside and examining the beaver skins packed on Bigfoot's mule, Casper quoted Bigfoot a price.

Bigfoot gave a low whistle. "Mister, you just bought you some beaver!" Bigfoot's eyes shined as Casper counted out the gold coins.

As Bigfoot headed back to his traplines, he chuckled to his mule. "Petunia, we might have skint that ol' boy... Oh well, that ain't none of my concern." The euphoria that Bigfoot felt caused him to let his guard down. He didn't realize he was being followed.

The gunshot echoed through the mountains. Anyone hearing it would have no reason to be concerned unless they thought it was Crow. Bigfoot's horse buckled at the knees, pitching the trapper over its head. Bigfoot staggered to his feet as he shouted, "Hold your fire, you durn fool! I ain't no elk!" Bigfoot never considered it to be Crow because it was too close to the fort and the soldiers. Bigfoot knew he was in trouble when a second shot struck Petunia. She gave a partial bray as she lay down on her side.

The trapper frantically grabbed for his rifle. Unfortunately, it was pinned beneath his horse. As Bigfoot engaged in a tug of war to pull out his rifle, a third shot rang out. The slug hit Bigfoot in the small of his back, causing paralysis. Bigfoot lay helpless as he wondered what would happen next. He was shocked when the face of Cheeves came into view. He asked his assailant, "Why?" The last thing Bigfoot saw in this life was the muzzle of Cheeves' gun just as he pulled the trigger. Cheeves stood for a while mesmerized by his handiwork. It fascinated him to watch the snow being stained red by Bigfoot's blood.

Cheeves plunked down the leather pouch of gold coins on Casper's desk. "Here's your money back, boss. There weren't no problems."

Casper greedily dumped out the contents. Cheeves noticed Casper carefully counting the coins to make sure none were missing. Casper looked up when he saw he was being watched. He explained, "Just making sure that trapper hadn't spent any yet." They both knew the real reason was to make sure none of the coins hadn't ended up in Cheeves' pocket.

No one knew Packy's real name. Packy was the moniker he went by. Packy trapped some, but only enough to buy whiskey. The part-time trapper spent most of his time swigging rotgut and sleeping it off in the back alleys of Laramie. It was also a mystery as when Packy had his last bath. Most of the mountain men weren't keen on personal hygiene. When asked when he was gonna get a bath, Packy responded, "I want to be sure griz can smell me! Most bears will vamoose iff'n they know a man is around. The way I figure it a good bath could get me killed. I'll just wait until I accidently fall in a crick. That happens sometimes when I've got too much of a snootful."

What mountain men may have lacked in cleanliness wasn't reflected in the care of their animals. A good horse or a mule could make the difference in survival in the mountains. Packy had a mule that he doted on. He would stroke his floppy ears. "Nathan, I reckon you is the best mule that ever lived." Normally Packy would walk as he pulled Nathan.

Packy was screeching as he galloped inside the gates of Fort Laramie, "They is dead! They is all dead!" Nathan slid to a stop. Packy burst through the door of Major Henderson's office, "They is dead! They is all dead!" Two soldiers each grabbed an arm of Packy's.

The major bolted up out of his chair. "Calm down, man! I can't understand you! Who is dead?"

Packy swallowed hard, "Bigfoot Fincher! His good horse..." Packy's voice broke as he continued, "...and Petunia...Why did they have to kill her? Petunia never hurt nobody!"

Major Henderson ordered a contingent of ten soldiers to accompany Packy back to the murder scene. They brought the body of Bigfoot back to the fort draped over the back of Nathan. Word spread like wildfire through Laramie of yet another cold-blooded killing.

A mob of angry citizens stormed into the fort. Soldiers blocked them from entering Major Henderson's office.

Angus Blackburn shouted, "Come out, Major! We got a right to know what you're doing about these murders! That's two good men and nothing's been done about it!"

In a few minutes, Henderson stepped out on the porch and motioned for quiet. He announced, "The United States Army will bring these law breakers to justice. We just need some time. I can assure you we are doing everything humanly possible. My men trailed Bigfoot's killer back to town but lost his tracks there. There were too many hoof prints."

Angus retorted, "While you take your time investigating, this killer is gunning down the good folks of Laramie."

The major wheeled around going back in his office.

When Bigfoot was buried, Kit and Jack were in attendance. Kit sighed. "Another one of my compadres dead. Ain't nobody doing shit about it either. I feel like I'm letting George and now Bigfoot down. If I ever get my hands on them who's done this…!"

Jack volunteered, "Maybe we need to be as sneaky as this sum bitch is. Why don't we leave town like we're going back to camp? I'll double back and see what I can find out."

Kit shrugged. "All right, just don't get yourself killed. I'm tired of burying folks."

Jack already had a strong notion who the killers were. That night Jack slipped back into Laramie. He crept up, squatting outside of Casper's office window. Most wouldn't have been able to hear the conversation, but Jack's keen hearing enabled him to savvy the muffled sounds.

Casper swore, "Dammit, Smythe. We should be prospering at a greater rate. Even acquiring that last load of pelts at no cost is not good enough. We must do better than that!"

Smythe responded, "Remember, boss, you said you didn't want to call me by my real name even when we're alone. You said that it might cause you to slip up."

Casper nodded. "You're right. I need to always call you Cheeves regardless of where we're at."

Cheeves continued, "The way I see it is these trappers are waiting for the American Fur Company to open back up. They feel some kind of stupid loyalty to George Atkins. I think we need to forget about trying to be on the up and up. I say we start robbing anyone we can."

Casper rubbed his head. "I don't know if that would be wise. It might not be good for the long term."

Cheeves snorted. "If we can't get it done in the short term, there ain't gonna be no long term!"

Casper replied, "What have you got in mind?"

Cheeves grinned. "There's a cabin at the edge of town. The rumor is the old man and old woman that live there have a secret gold strike. They say that the old man pays for everything in gold dust. I say I should pay them a visit tonight to see if the rumor is true."

Casper smirked. "A social call might be just the thing."

When Cheeves circled out back of the office to retrieve his horse, he was viciously struck on the head. Cheeves lapsed into unconsciousness without seeing his attacker. He came to in total darkness with a searing headache. Cheeves realized he was draped over a horse and there was a sack over his head. He became queasy when Cheeves realized that the sack was soaked in blood, most likely his own. He cried out, "Who are you? Where are you taking me?" Another blow from a rifle butt put him out again.

Jack and Kit had recently noticed some bear scat that could only be Slew Foot's. Kit pointed it out while nervously scanning the trees for the mammoth grizzly. Kit whispered, "Ain't no griz can shit as much as Slew Foot. Let's get out of here." Jack had made a mental note of the location.

Jack knew that Slew Foot might still be in that area or he might have moved on. Jack thought to himself, *Whether that ol' bear is around or not, this sum bitch is going to get a taste of Apache justice. I considered George and Bigfoot my friends too.* Jack jerked Cheeves off the horse with his hands still tied behind his back. Cheeves landed with a grunt.

When Jack removed the sack, Cheeves began blinking, trying to clear his vision. "Where are we? Don't you know that kidnapping is against the law? You could go to jail for this!"

Jack's eyes narrowed. "You murdered two friends of mine. There doesn't seem to be enough evidence to put you in jail. As an Apache, I can't allow that. My father, Great Hawk, taught me better than that. He told me that your enemies would only grow stronger if left unpunished."

Jack cocked his Hawken. When he pulled the trigger, the ball tore out Cheeves' right knee. The kneecap flew one direction and the knee socket flew another. Cheeves screamed in a white-hot pain that was unlike anything he had ever experienced.

Off in the distance, Slew Foot lifted his head at the sound of the gunshot. The grizzly honed in on the shrieking. It was a prey animal that was ripe for the taking. Slew Foot clacked his teeth together as he lumbered with deceptive speed towards the easy meal. Jack had long since galloped from the scene when the big bear spied the withering man flopping around on the ground.

To Cheeves' horror, the size of Slew Foot blotted out the sky. With his hands still tied behind him, Cheeves couldn't even put up an ineffectual defense by shielding his face with his hands. Slew Foot untied his hands when he ripped off one of his arms. The huge grizzly crunched the arm into bite-sized pieces. With his muzzle now covered in blood, Slew Foot buried his jaws into the soft belly of his victim. Cheeves screamed again when he watched the grizzly chew up the steaming intestines. Mercifully, death claimed the misspent life of Archibald Smythe. Slew Foot rolled in the remains, delighting in his feast. The bear's coat ended up with a light frosting of blood and gore.

Kit was incredulous. Upon hearing the details, Kit exclaimed, "You did what? You actually fed Cheeves to Slew Foot? I ain't never heard of such a thing!"

Jack shrugged. "I ain't for sure for happened. I didn't want to hang around to see. To tell you the truth, that bear spooks me too."

In a couple of days, Jack cautiously led Kit back to where he left Cheeves. All they found were a few bits of cloth and half a skull. The ground was torn up from Slew Foot's party. Kit shivered as he whispered, "Well, I'll be damned. I reckon I've seen it all now!" After Kit told a few of his friends, the story quickly spread among the mountain men and the Laramie community. The retelling of the tale even made it to the Crows. Scar remarked, "To kill such a man would cover me in glory." Scar screamed his war cry in a vow to kill the mountain man.

That day of Cheeves' demise marked the beginning of the Legend of Jack Flint, Mountain Man.

Kit remarked, "I'm glad you got Cheeves. He had the eyes of a timber rattler. But what about Casper? That sum bitch needs to pay for what he's done!"

Jack grinned, "I ain't forgot about him. I was saving him for you. I figured you would want to settle the score personally."

Kit scowled, "I damn sure do!"

It had been three days since Cheeves had vanished. Casper had started to sweat after one day. Day three saw the outlaw in a panic. He tried to hole up in the fort, begging Major Henderson, "Major, the army has got to protect me! There's a killer on the loose! I know he's after me!"

The major responded, "What have you got in common with the deaths of George Atkins and Bigfoot Fincher? Unless there's some kind of connection, I don't think you are any more at risk than anybody else."

Casper pleaded, "I can feel it in my bones. I'm going to be next!"

Henderson shook his head. "Sorry, I don't have enough men anyway without assigning them based on a groundless suspicion." Casper grabbed the major's arm. Henderson jerked away as he commanded the soldier standing just inside the door, "Sergeant, escort this man out of the fort!"

Word got out that Casper was willing to pay any man to take him back East. He was refused at every turn. One trapper responded, "You found your way out here. You should be able to find your way back!" Casper passed out due to too much whiskey and a lack of sleep. He was awakened by being roughly shaken. "Casper, wake up! Wake up, damn you!" As Casper groggily regained consciousness, he made out a dim figure standing over him in the darkened room. He coughed, "I can pay you whatever you want to get me back to civilization!"

The figure laughed. "Ain't we civilized enough for you? Besides you got a few things to answer for. George Atkins and Bigfoot Fincher were good friends of mine. You murdered them. The law of the mountains says you have to pay for that."

Casper sputtered, "I-I've never heard about any mountain law. Besides I never touched those men. It was Cheeves! I told me not to do it. Just ask him! He can tell you!"

Kit laughed. "I don't think I can do that. I've never heard bear shit talk before."

Casper whined, "Please… please… I have money and pelts. You can have it all! Just don't hurt me."

When Kit didn't immediately answer him, Casper thought he might get the chance to live. Those hopes were dashed when he felt the sharp blade of a skinning knife slice deeply across his throat. Casper tried to talk, but blood was all that came out. Kit announced, "Well, that takes care of that."

Jack was back deeper in the shadows. He stepped forward. "No! That's not that. An Apache would never let that… be that." Jack pulled his own knife while stripping Casper of all his clothes. With the practiced cuts learned in his youth, Jack gutted and quartered Casper. He scattered the body parts over the accumulated beaver skins. Jack looked approvingly at his work. "Now that… is that!"

Kit was speechless until they started back to camp. He looked at Jack like he had never seen him before. "Boy, I hope I never do nothing to piss you off."

Jack grinned. "You are my friend. That means something to an Apache. Only our enemies have anything to fear."

The details of Casper Fortenberry's death spread throughout the Wind River Mountains. Most mountain men had seen and heard just about everything. None knew of anything like this. In the Shoshone village, one warrior said to another, "Everything about that tale reminds me of something my grandfather told me long ago. At one time Grandfather lived down below among the Apache. He said the Apache would quarter their enemies. It doesn't make any sense. I've never heard of Apache being this far north."

Buffalo Bob was upset. He declared, "It ain't enough I got to worry about soldiers, that damn Slew Foot and now I got to watch for this Jack Flint! Maybe I'll just put a bullet through the head of ol' Kit. Maybe that will be enough to get Flint to drop his guard so I can get a clear shot at him too." Bob laughed at the thought of wolves picking the bones of Kit and Jack clean.

Kit was skillfully rebaiting a trap when the bullet buzzed his head, taking off a piece of ear. Kit immediately dropped the trap, rolling through the snow to the protection of an aspen. He huddled behind the tree, his eyes searching for whoever shot at him. There was no movement for several minutes. Kit finally heard a horse in the distance as it was being ridden away. The pain of his injured ear suddenly hit him. Kit vigorously rubbed snow on his bloody ear, "Sum bitch! That hurts!" Kit walked in the direction of the horse that had carried Kit's attacker away. After examining the hoof prints, Kit swore, "Damn you, Bob! I know you done this! Best keep a good check on your backtrail cause I'm a-coming!"

Kit tracked down Jack. As he slung his extra traps across Jack's pack horse, Kit spat, "I need you to tend to things for a spell. That polecat, Buffalo Bob, took a shot at me this morning. I'm going after him and settle his hash once and for all."

Jack noticed a jagged piece of Kit's ear was missing. Jack grinned. "It looks like he's trying to take you apart a piece at a time. Maybe I ought to tag along to make sure you come back with everything you started out with."

Kit snorted. "He got lucky. Besides they ain't no way I can't handle somebody the likes of Bob. And I certainly don't need no help from a young'un like you still wet behind the ears."

Kit was careful trailing Bob. He knew Bob would be checking over his shoulder. Buffalo Bob was fit to be tied. "How in the hell did I miss that shot? I had that damn Kit Bridger dead to rights. It must be this gun. The tree limb I hit the other day must have knocked it off of plumb. Damn the luck!" For two days Bob tried to throw Kit off his scent. Finally, after the second night of making a cold camp, Bob's nerves couldn't take the thought of Kit showing up unexpectedly with blood in his eye.

Bob chuckled to himself. "There's no one smarter than me. I'll just set a trap for Bridger that he won't expect. Let's see him get out of that." The more Bob thought about his plan, the more insane his laugh became.

Once Bob knew he was in Crow territory, the hair kept standing up on the back of his neck. He couldn't get it to stop no matter how many times he shivered. Bob understood his life was in great danger by even being in Crow territory, but his plan required that he take that risk. He was more afraid of Kit tracking him down. Bob set up an ambush on a well-used game trail. In a few hours, a war party of seven Crows came trotting up the trail. Scar had sent them out on a scouting mission looking for whites or Shoshone to capture or kill. Bob sighted in on the lead brave. His ball crushed the Crow's chest, blasting him back over his pony's rump. The rest of the Indians immediately scattered. Bob wasted no time mounting his horse and galloping back from direction he came.

Kit was also extra cautious, realizing he was in Crow country. He cocked his good ear at a distant noise. As it got closer, Kit recognized the sound of a galloping horse. He moved into the cover of a dense thicket. Kit's horse neighed at the oncoming equine. Kit gripped the horse's nose, whispering, "Be quiet, you durn fool." Even at a full gallop, Bob's horse returned the greeting. Bob reined his horse in the direction of where its ears were pointed. He hoped it was Kit's horse. Finding Kit at this instant was key to his plan. Kit was immobilized by the sight of the man he had been tracking rush by Kit's hidden position.

Kit stepped out from the thicket, his mouth gaping in amazement as he watched the fleeing Bob. To further add to Kit's confusion, Bob was cackling hysterically as he rode by. Kit was swiftly brought back to the here and now by the screeching Crow warriors in hot pursuit of the killer of one of their people. Kit tried to conceal himself again, but it was no use. The Crows had already seen him.

There was an unrest in Jack's spirit after Kit left. Jack knew it meant something. Jack thought, *I know that the old man will be pissed if he catches me following him, but ignoring my gut might put Kit in danger...besides, an Apache can trail someone without them knowing it.* Jack laughed. *Or at least I think I can.*

Jack quickly lifted his head while following Kit's trail. Jack had noticed that Kit's tracks were on top of another set of tracks. Jack figured they were Buffalo Bob's. Jack was astonished to see a rider galloping toward a sheer cliff while screeching insanely. Bob's twisted mind had convinced him that going over the edge was his only hope to escape. Jack saw the rider viciously spurring the horse, driving it over the cliff. Bob and his horse separated in flight as they tumbled toward the rocks below. The horse was squealing in fright.

Jack hadn't completely recovered from viewing that incredible spectacle when his attention was snapped toward the sounds of Indian war whoops. Jack's gut told him that it had to be Kit. Jack heeled his horse in the direction of the conflict.

Kit triggered the Hawken killing a Crow, but there were still five left. Kit had wedged himself into the branches of an Evergreen. His backside was protected, but he had no path to escape. With the practice from countless times, Kit reloaded his rifle. One of the warriors was within a few feet when a ball from the Hawken took out a big chunk of his belly. The four remaining braves swarmed the hated mountain man, slashing with their knives. They were too close for Kit to use his rifle as a club. Instead Kit brandished his own knife, growling, "Come on, you red heathen! Who wants to be next to go to the happy hunting ground? Come on!"

After a hand-to-hand struggle, the Crows pinned Kit to the ground. There was one on each arm and one sitting on Kit's legs. Kit watched stoically as the fourth warrior raised his knife for a killing thrust. Kit's final thought was, *I hope Jack will be all right.* Before the knife could descend, the Crow's head exploded. It was blown apart by a musket ball.

A figure flashed into view, knocking over one of the Indians. Jack's knife cut open the throat of the Crow who had been on Kit's legs. Jack swiftly shed the body, pouncing on another brave. He thrust his knife into the unguarded neck of the Crow and twisted it. The Crow's eyes rolled back in his head as he gurgled his last. Meanwhile, Kit located his knife, stabbing the remaining Crow who was stubbornly still clenching his arm. After two more thrusts into the Crow's belly, Kit made sure he was dead by slitting his throat.

Kit leaned back against the tree in exhaustion. Jack grinned, "You okay?"

Kit stammered, "I-It… Where the hell did you come from?"

Jack smiled. "I just figured a man of your age might need some help… so I tagged along."

Kit retorted, "See, that's the kind of bullshit I figured I'd get from you! As it so happens, I didn't need you to butt in! I had them Injuns exactly where I wanted them. You just made a mess by mixing in!"

Jack laughed. "Now why didn't I think of that? 'Cause it looked like to me your scalp was fixin' to belong to one of them Crows. That'll teach me to believe my lying eyes."

On the ride back to camp, Kit muttered, "Okay, maybe I did need a little something extra back there. Thanks for helping out."

Jack replied, "I need you around as long as Slew Foot is alive. If we're together, I don't need to outrun him. I just need to outrun you."

Kit retorted, "Shut up!" In a minute, Kit continued, "And don't you think you went a little too far with them Crow bodies?"

Jack shrugged. "Our enemies need to fear us."

When the scouting party became three days overdue, Scar took a couple of his warriors and went to search for them. Even as brutal as the Crow chieftain was, he was slackjawed at the carnage of his scouts' last stand. All six of his braves had been quartered with the parts scattered. The ground was stained red with blood. All had been scalped, their hair burned in a small fire. Scar cut his arms as if in mourning. The truth was he felt little sorrow about the deaths of his men. What sent him into a rage was the perceived disrespect that someone had shown him. His pride couldn't tolerate it. He vowed, "As surely as the Great Spirit lives, I will destroy the killer of my people!" His war cries echoed through the mountains.

Kit maintained a friendly relationship with the Shoshone by occasionally visiting their village. His friendship with them began a number of years previous when Kit found a young boy, wounded from a bear attack. The boy was at death's door. Kit nursed him back to health. The boy was Little Star, son of the Shoshone chief, Long Knife. When Kit rode into the Shoshone camp with Little Star riding behind him, Kit became a man of stature with the Indians. The entire village had searched for the missing boy, but a fierce blizzard wiped out all traces of him. The feast with Kit as the man of honor lasted most of a week. The Shoshone would defend Kit as if he were one of their own.

After telling Jack the background story, Kit said, "We need to go visit the Shoshone. I ain't seen them for a spell.

They're about the only family I got. Besides, they need to get to know you. One day they might come in right handy. Family's always good to have."

Jack responded, "I'd rather have Indian friends than white ones anyways. With Indians, a man knows where he stands. With a white man, he's doing one thing and saying another."

The entire village crowded around, greeting Kit. A smiling Long Knife motioned. "Get down, my friend. We will eat and smoke."

Kit replied, "Thank you, Chief. This here is sorta my adopted son, Jack."

Long Knife smiled. "Welcome, Jack. You will eat and smoke with us."

As the three men sat cross-legged in Long Knife's teepee, a girl entered the flap, bringing them food. Jack was stunned. He had never seen a more beautiful young woman. She was tall and willowy with waist-length black hair that shone like a raven's wing.

Kit snickered under his breath, "Get them eyeballs back in your head. That's the chief's daughter, Mountain Mist." Kit and Long Knife continued to talk while Jack kept an eye on the tent flap for Mountain Mist's return. Kit asked the chief, "I don't see Little Star. Where is he?"

Long Knife responded, "He is out hunting with some of the other young men. He will be back in a few days."

When Kit and Long Knife began smoking, Jack took one turn before announcing, "I will step outside for a little air." Jack walked around the village. He was mostly greeted by warm expressions and nods. There were a few suspicious looks. Jack ignored them.

He saw Mountain Mist coming back from the forest with a load of firewood. Jack smiled. "Can I help you with that?"

Mountain Mist ducked her head in embarrassment. "This is a woman's chore. A man should not do it."

Jack shrugged. "I don't mind. I doubt if another man will call me out about it when they find out who I am?"

Mountain Mist giggled. "And who are you? Am I supposed to know this?"

Jack grinned. "I am the Feeder of Slew Foot and the Killer of Crows."

Mountain Mist gasped. "I have heard of such a man. You are him?"

Now it was Jack's turn to be embarrassed for bragging. He decided he didn't care. Jack would do anything to find favor with the beautiful Shoshone girl. Jack didn't answer, pretending to be looking at a couple of twittering birds in the trees.

When they had finished smoking, Kit asked Long Knife, "You still having trouble with the Crows?"

Long Knife curled his upper lip. "The Crows should be killed, especially Scar. He leads a charmed life. Just when we think we have him, he seems to disappear. A single hunter from our village is no longer safe. I have ordered that our hunters must travel in pairs. I think it's gotten worse since your son killed that war party."

Kit's eyes widened. "You heard about that?"

Long Knife replied, "Your son has already established himself as a great warrior. We sing songs about the Killer of Crows and the Feeder of Slew Foot around our campfires. You must be very proud of him."

A stunned Kit cleared his throat. "I am proud of the boy. I am just surprised that so many have heard of Jack already."

Little Star and his best friend, Silent One, were creeping as they tracked the deer. The boys grew up together, running naked through the village as toddlers. The young Shoshone were usually inseparable. Silent One blamed himself for not being with Little Star when he was almost killed by a bear. No one was happier when Kit returned Little Star to his family.

Little Star grinned as he cut his eyes at his friend. They were both thinking the same thing—how good the deer would taste. Little Star was stunned when an arrow thudded into Silent One. Neither one of the boys had detected the Crows waiting in ambush. The deer spooked when the stillness was broken by a chorus of Crow war cries. Little Star launched his nocked arrow at the diving Crow. The arrow passed through the neck of his enemy.

Before Little Star could nock another arrow, he was overwhelmed by the attacking Crows. Long Knife's son put up a valiant fight. He grunted as each knife thrust penetrated his body. In the end, his life blood stained the snow as Little Star slipped into death.

Star commanded, "The scalps are mine!" Fear of their leader kept the other Crows from complaining even though they had all participated in the successful killing of the Shoshone warriors. Scar took great pleasure in lifting Little Star's hair, removing the scalp with the sharp edge of his skinning knife. Scar brandished the scalp in the air as he rejoiced, "The son of Long Knife has fallen!"

When Little Star and Silent One had not returned to the village, Long Knife did not send out a band of warriors but led the search party himself. The chief could not dispel the uneasiness he felt about his son being missing. An advance scout came back with a storm cloud for a face. Long Knife knew instantly what it meant. He drummed his pony's ribs urging more speed.

The scalped bodies of Little Star and Silent One rocked the normally stoic Shoshone. War whoops of rage were screamed. Long Knife's response was measured. He was torn between the grief of his son's death and his responsibilities as the chief. The village erupted into the trilling of sorrow when the bodies were brought in. The young warriors were clamoring for revenge. They screeched, "Death to the Crows! Their scalps will hang from our lodge poles!"

Long Knife raised both arms to speak. When the tribe became quiet, Long Knife announced, "My blade thirsts for the blood of the killers of our people. I burn for the pursuit and deaths of our enemies. But such an attack on the Crow village would result in many deaths in the Shoshone nation. I will not sacrifice my people in a foolish attack. This is the same reason the Crows will not attack our village. Their losses would be unacceptable to them… I have spoken." The chief returned to his teepee to weep over the body of his son.

Kit and Jack walked their horses into the Shoshone village. Word had gotten around regarding the death of Little Star. Kit greeted Long Knife. "My heart is heavy over the passing of Little Star."

Long Knife nodded in appreciation. "We must continue in the land of the living. Come to my teepee, my friend. We will eat and smoke."

Jack didn't follow the men. His eyes searched for Mountain Mist. She was coming back from the never-ending search for firewood. Mountain Mist did not have the same twinkle in her eye that Jack had seen before. Jack stepped in front of her. "I am sorry about your brother. What can I do?"

Mountain Mist fiercely retorted, "Bring me the scalp of Scar!" She brushed past Jack, headed for her teepee.

When Jack and Kit left the village to return to camp, Kit noticed the brooding look on Jack's face. He commented, "Jack, I don't like what I'm seeing. I hope you ain't getting some fool notion that might get yourself killed."

Jack shrugged. "I haven't figured out exactly what I'm going to do, but I'm going to do something."

Kit muttered, "Oh, hell."

The next morning, Jack said to Kit, "Partner, I need for you to take care of our trapline for a spell."

Kit's brow furrowed, "Why? What are you going to do?"

Jack responded, "I'm going to get the lay of the land. What I find out will determine what I do."

Kit replied, "So you're going without me? What if you need some help? And you probably will! What happens then?"

Jack smiled, "And then I die... I don't want to take you down with me. I'm leaving my horse. Being by myself gives me the best chance of being undetected."

Kit spat, "Go ahead! Get yourself kilt! It won't be on my head!"

Jack knew that Kit was just concerned for his wellbeing. Jack smiled again.

Kit growled, "All this over a girl you hardly know. Damn kid."

The time for talk was over. The only weapons Jack took was his bow, arrows and skinning knife. A gun made too much noise. Jack's Apache upbringing had taught him stealth, being one with his surroundings. Even at his young age he was the best in his tribe at hiding his tracks. Jack knew the general direction of the Crow village. He whispered to himself, "I will bring you what you want, Mountain Mist, or I will die trying."

Jack took a week to scout the Crow camp. He lived off squirrels and rabbits that he could silently kill with his bow. Jack devoured their raw flesh. Warm weather had melted most of the snow. Jack drank from the natural springs that had thawed and were now flowing. Jack became familiar with the Crow warriors and their women. He learned everything about them, down to what time a day and where they defecated.

Jack rose swiftly out of one of the last concealing snowbanks to drive his knife through the top of the skull of the squatting warrior. At the same time his hand fastened around the mouth of his victim, muffling any sounds of dying.

A cry rang out when the Crow woman found her missing husband, lying in his own feces. The Crow warriors quickly responded. They filled the air with war hoops at the atrocity.

One warrior exclaimed, "There are no tracks! This must be the work of a demon!" The Crows shrank back in fear.

When Scar arrived, he smirked disgustedly. "It is no demon! It is a Shoshone taking revenge for the ones who fell under my knife!"

Another warrior asked, "If it is Shoshone, where are the tracks?"

Scar ignored the question. He took most of his warriors and searched the ground surrounding the village. There were no guards around the camp because Scar felt that no intruder would be foolish enough to attack the tribe.

Finding no trace of the killer made even Scar feel uneasy. This was the first part of Jack's plan. He wanted the Crow to be concerned that he was not a creature of this world, but one sent from the supernatural. Jack wanted to sow the confusion that would affect their logic. Jack silently laughed hidden in a tree only fifty yards away.

The Crow woman was gathering firewood. She walked directly under the tree where Jack was perched. Just as he was taught by the Apache, Jack did not see a woman. He saw an enemy. Jack also knew that if he was captured the woman would join and perhaps lead his torture. The squaw was knocked unconscious when the full weight of Jack landed on her head and shoulders. A few rapid cuts from Jack's knife sliced open her throat and separated her from her scalp. Jack cast the bloody scalp on the woman's body. That act told the Crow that he was a great warrior and wouldn't stoop to decorate his lodgepole with the hair of a woman.

The two women who went searching for the missing squaw shrilly trilled with despair at the discovery of the body. This time Scar was the first one on the scene. He commanded the arriving warriors, "Scatter and find this Shoshone dog. The woman's blood is fresh!" After hours of searching produced no results, Scar vowed, "I will kill this murderer of my people! Tomorrow I will find him and return with his scalp. All will sing my praises around the campfire that night!" Scar went out by himself. He did not want to share the glory of the kill with anyone else.

The arrow from Jack's bow struck the ground between Scar's feet. The Crow chieftain jumped back in alarm as he clutched his knife cutting the air in a defensive posture. Jack stepped out from behind a pine tree. Jack laughed. "It would have been an easy matter to have put that arrow in your heart. You are not the great warrior you claim to be! I have seen women who would be harder to kill than you! You are one who kills from hiding. We will see if you can kill face to face."

Scar bared his teeth. "You are no Shoshone! Who are you?"

Jack laughed again, "I think you know who I am. I am the Feeder of Slew Foot and the Killer of Crows!"

Scar grimaced slightly at the confirmation that his fear was realized. Scar shrieked his war cry as he charged Jack. When Jack sidestepped the Crow, he slashed at his enemy. His blade left a deep gap on Scar's face. The white of the bone could be seen through the red blood. Scar quickly recovered and rushed Jack again. This time Jack's knife sliced a part of Scar's windpipe. The Crow staggered, going to his knees. His breath partially bubbled foam from his throat.

Rage took over as Scar screamed, "I will cut you into pieces for the wolves! I am Scar, chief of the Crow!"

Jack shrugged. "Your time as their chief is almost finished. Can you die better than you lived?" Jack went from being defensive to attacking. Jack's thrust gaped the Crow's throat. Jack snatched Scar's knife throwing it into a thicket. As the life slowly drained from Scar, Jack scalped him while he was still living. The Crow chieftain's screams reverberated through the mountains.

Jack strode through the Shoshone village. Several of the warriors looked questioningly at Long Knife. Long Knife slightly shook his head as he looked approvingly at Jack. Jack stopped at Mountain Mist's teepee, calling out, "Mountain Mist, I have done what you have asked."

Mountain Mist stuck out her head through the tent flap. When she saw what Jack was carrying, she ran to him. The twinkle was back in her eyes, "Jack, you have done it! You have avenged my brother!"

Jack thrust the scalp skyward. The Apache war battle cry was not the same as the Shoshone, but the Shoshone joined him in shouting.

When the din of the noise quieted down, Jack grinned as he offered the scalp to Mountain Mist, "I make a gift of Scar's hair to you."

Mountain Mist lowered her head. "That is not my place to show a warrior's prize."

As the war whoops split the quiet again, Long Knife raised his hands. He waited for silence from his people. The chief announced, "Two suns from now, the Feeder of Slew Foot and the Killer of the Crows will become a blood brother to the Shoshone!" Mountain Mist may have trilled the loudest.

Kit was puttering around camp, tending to several traps that needed to be fixed. He jumped when a loud voice boomed out of the thin air, "So this is how you take care of our trapline? Are the beaver using our traps to scratch their backs?"

Kit swore as Jack showed himself, "Son.. of.. a.. bitch!"

Jacked laughed heartily. "I hope you haven't written me off as a lost cause."

Kit grabbed Jack by the arms as he inspected him. "I don't see no holes… Are you all right?"

Jack replied, "I'm fine. By the way, have you got any duds for a party?"

Kit was confused. "What party? Now wait just a damn minute! What happened between you and Scar?"

Jack pulled the scalp from his belt and tossed it at Kit. "He won't be killing any more Shoshone."

Kit turned the scalp over in his hands, examining it. In a minute, Kit exclaimed, "What party?"

Jack chuckled. "Oh, you know. The one where I become a blood brother to the Shoshone."

Kit scratched his head. "Well, I'll be a suck-egg mule. I'll say one thing for you, boy. You damn sure are entertaining."

As Kit and the entire tribe looked on, Long Knife slit the palm of his hand, then Jack's. The chief clasped their hands together, blood mixing with blood, and announced, "From this day forward this warrior won't be like a Shoshone, he will be a Shoshone!" The war whoops from the Shoshone were deafening. Even Kit was shouting. Jack thrust his bloody hand in the air and joined in with an Apache war cry. Jack noticed the last woman to stop trilling was Mountain Mist.

Jack and Kit stayed with the Indians for four days in celebration. On their ride back to their own camp, Jack asked, "So how does a man marry with the Shoshone?"

Kit burst out guffawing. "Boy, iff'n you is asking what I think you're asking, you might be better getting hitched with Slew Foot! That's the chief's daughter. She ain't no ordinary gal."

Jack retorted, "Like I said, how do I do it?"

Kit sputtered, "W-well, I guess the first thing you would need to talk to Long Knife. Knowing how much the old man thinks of that girl, I you might lose your hair then and there."

Jack sat cross-legged facing Long Knife in his teepee. The chief had noticed the looks that had passed between his daughter and Jack. He had a notion what Jack wanted. Long Knife ordered his wives and Mountain Mist, "Leave us." Long Knife sat stone-faced, staring at Jack.

Despite facing down Crows and grizzly bears, Jack squirmed a little. "Well, you see… Chief Long Knife, I want to marry Mountain Mist." Jack watched, concerned that the chief was going to reach for his skinning knife.

Long Knife asked, "How would you pay for her?" Jack carefully laid out the scalp on the blanket between them. The suitor replied, "I will make a gift to you of the hair from the Crow who murdered your son."

Long Knife's stare shifted from Jack to the scalp laying before him. After several minutes went by, Jack nervously said, "And if that's not enough, you just name the price… I will pay anything for Mountain Mist."

Long Knife picked up the scalp, looking at Jack. "This is enough. I don't know if any of my warriors could have paid this."

Long Knife got to his feet, left the teepee, but came back in with his daughter. He asked Mountain Mist, "This man wants you to join him in marriage. Would you have him?"

Jack's heart soared when Mountain Mist immediately nodded her head in agreement.

Jack was due back for the ceremony in a week. In the meantime, Mountain Mist built them a teepee with the help of the women of the tribe. Just before leaving camp for the marriage vows, Kit remarked, "Last chance to back out. 'Course you'd probably have to go to Mexico."

Jack laughed. "I have no intention to back out. I've wanted Mountain Mist from the first time I saw her."

Kit sighed. "Well, I guess that rips it. You're a goner."

On the ride to the Shoshone village, Kit added, "Are we still gonna be trapping partners? That girl will have y'all a teepee for you to live in."

Jack responded, "We'll stay there for a spell, but I'll be coming back to trap. I might bring her with me."

Kit snorted. "That's a damn fool idea. We don't have a cabin or a place for her to stay."

Jack shrugged. "We can sleep out under the stars if need be. Besides, she's Indian. We Indians can get by."

Kit smirked. "Well, technically, you ain't no Indian. I just hope the white boy in you don't come out."

Jack grinned all the way to the village.

Mountain Mist was dressed in deerskin trimmed with fringes. She wore a beaded headband. Jack thought he had never seen anything so beautiful. Jack and Mountain Mist stood in front of Long Knife next to the campfire. Long Knife draped each of them in a blue blanket. The entire village looked on as their chief intoned, "This man and woman have agreed to walk the path of life together." The Shoshone shouted their approval. Long Knife removed the two blue blankets and wrapped them together in a single white blanket. Long Knife continued, "May you find the true path of the Shoshone!"

Jack and Mountain Mist walked hand in hand to their teepee accompanied by the trills of the tribe. The chief turned to Kit. "Let us go to my teepee to smoke."

Jack had never known a woman. Mountain Mist had never known a man. They spent the week exploring the delights of their bodies. Mountain Mist would occasionally leave the teepee to bring back food. One night they joined the tribe around the campfire.

Kit, who had stayed around trading tales with Long Knife, remarked to Jack, "Well, I see you're still alive. I was starting to have my doubts. I'm glad I didn't have to gather up a few of the boys and come in after you."

Jack smiled. "Come on, old man, that would have been way too much excitement for somebody your age. You might have been the one to die."

Kit turned red. "Shut up! Damn kid."

The Crow finally decided to look for Scar. Six warriors left the camp to search. When they found the desecrated body of their war chief, they wailed in mourning. Their sorrow was not as intense as one might have expected. The truth was while Scar was revered for his ferociousness in battle, he was genuinely disliked by most of the tribe. His disfavor was rooted in putting his own selfish interests ahead of his people. Most considered him invincible so it was quite a shock to the Crow. No one had considered who would succeed him as chief until his lifeless body was brought in.

The second most despised person in the Crow village was a young warrior named Snake Eye. Snake Eye was a son of Scar. Scar had raped a woman in the village. When Spring Lilly became with child, she confronted him. "Chief Scar, the baby I am carrying is yours."

Scar mocked her. "You don't know who the father is. You've been with many braves! Any one of them could be the father."

Spring Lilly protested, "That is not true! You are the only man I have been with. This child is yours!"

Scar slapped her so hard he knocked her down. He kicked her several times in the stomach. Some thought he was trying to end her pregnancy. Scar threatened, "If you continue to spread lies about me, I will cut you open and feed it to the wolves!" Scar laughed when the baby was born. He smirked,

"What an ugly child! He has a head and eyes of a snake. He shall be known as Snake Eye!"

When the tribal elders were discussing who should be the new chief, Snake Eye strode out of the shadows into the light of the campfire. He proclaimed, "I am the best choice for chief. Everyone knows who my father was. I have the same strong blood in my veins."

Red Fox objected. "You are not your father. I have more experience than you. I should be chief."

When no one else claimed the right to be chief, Snake Eye slyly smiled. He said to Red Fox, "We will settle this the Crow way. We will fight for the honor to be chief." Normally, combat between Crows consisted of the opponents facing each other and a third party declaring when to fight. Snake Eye didn't want to take any chances. He attacked Red Fox before he was ready. Snake Eye's knife repeatedly sank into the belly of Red Fox. Red Fox staggered and fell to the ground, his blood pooling under him.

One of the braves protested, "That was not right! Red Fox was not expecting to fight yet. There is no honor in that!"

Snake Eye shrugged. "Why is it my fault that Red Fox was not prepared? He was too foolish to be chief." The sudden and vicious assault on the unsuspecting Crow muted the rest of the tribe. Most thought to themselves that their new chief was the same as their old chief.

The smell of elk wafted to the nose of Slew Foot. Saliva began to drip from his fangs triggered by the thought of sinking his teeth in the delicious flesh. A cow elk and her calf carelessly fed down the ridge. The cow went into a full-fledged panic at the sound of the grizzly's roar as he charged.

She ran into several trees in her hysterical flight from danger. The calf was not so lucky as it tripped on a root, crashing in a pile at the base of a tall pine. Slew Foot was on the calf before it could recover its feet. His jaws clamped shut on the middle of the young elk's back. Slew Foot snapped its spine before tossing it in the air. The mammoth bear roared again in celebration of its kill. The helpless calf was bleating, calling for its mother. Slew Foot responded by slapping the calf around with his massive paws. He enjoyed playing with the young elk before devouring it in half a dozen bites.

After a long and arduous trip from Mississippi, Randy and Betsy Unger decided to leave the wagon train on the Oregon Trail. Randy had heard good thing about the business potential in Laramie. The wagon master did his best to discourage him. "Mr. Unger, it's not wise to leave the protection of the train. You are open to Indian attacks. Them Crow are nobody to fool with. Plus, there's lots of grizzlies around. You and the missus need to stay with us."

Randy shook his head. "I appreciate it, but I'm not a farmer or rancher like most of the rest. I aim to open a dry goods place in Laramie. Clerkin' is what I know."

As the covered wagon lurched up the trail to Laramie, they left the sights and sounds of the line of wagons occupied by people they had become friends with over the past months. Betsy sighed deeply. "Honey, you know how much I love you. I will follow you anywhere, but I have this bad feeling… Like something terrible is going to happen."

Randy smiled as he patted his wife's arm. "It's just the change from leaving the others. It would make anyone nervous. Honestly, everything is going to be all right. I have my rifle and pistol. That'll take care of Indians and bears. Don't worry so much."

Betsy tried to force a smile. "Okay, if you say so..." There was now an ache in the pit of her stomach.

Slew Foot sat on his haunches like a huge dog. He squinted in an effort to identify the oncoming object. The grizzly began to sniff the air as a bear relies on the sense of smell more than their eyesight. Slew Foot remained motionless except for the slight flick of one ear. Randy thought he saw movement out of the corner of his eye. The man started to squint too in an attempt to locate the source of the movement. To his horror a massive bear began to materialize through the trees. At first Randy was sure it was his imagination. Reality set in when the bear bellowed with its teeth snapping as he charged.

Slew Foot rammed the side of the wagon, flipping it on its side as Randy was trying to prime his old muzzleloader. It was total chaos as Randy, Betsy and both horses trapped in their harness, screamed in one voice. Betsy was shrieking, "Randy! Randy!" Randy was scrambling on the ground desperately searching for his lost guns. Betsy fainted, which prevented her from seeing the raging bear chomping off one of Randy's arms at the shoulder. Blood spurted from the stump. He was still conscious as he watched Slew Foot bite into Betsy's belly. The grizzly devoured her intestines and internal organs with one monstrous gulp. The bear savored the sweet, steaming meat. Slew Foot tossed Betsy's body like a rag doll.

As the grizzly busied himself with disemboweling the squealing horses, Randy was trying to drag himself away from the horrifying scene. He was whispering feebly, "No...

no… please, no." Even though his crawling was in slow motion, Slew Foot bristled at the thought of his prey getting away. He quickly caught up to Randy, slapping the would-be store clerk with a giant paw. Randy flew twenty feet through the air as he crashed against the base of an aspen. The grizzly finished the kill by ripping off Randy's head. Slew Foot roared his satisfaction at the prospect of eating on the flesh of the settlers and horses for several days.

John Brown had trapped in the Wind River range for close to ten years. He was a seasoned mountain man. John had survived Indian attacks and grizzly charges. John once told Kit, "I ain't scared of much. I know how to take care of myself, but I have to admit I get spooked if I think Slew Foot is in the area. I don't know if he's real or a demon sent by the Great Spirit to avenge the red men losing their land to the white man."

Kit retorted, "Nah, he ain't no demon taking revenge. He's kilt as many Injuns as he has whites. But I know what you mean. I don't cotton to grizzlies much to begin with. That goes double for that sum bitch!"

John's mind drifted a little that morning as he was checking his traps. Normally, John paid close attention to his surroundings. He understood that danger could be around the next tree. The sight of the trap with only a remnant of a beaver's paw in it, sharpened his attention. The only thing left of the beaver was the red stain of its blood on the ground. John also knew it would take a big bear to swallow the beaver's skull. His mind went immediately to Slew Foot. John muttered, "Oh, hell," as he slowly backed up. John attempted to retrace his steps. Fear rose up in John's stomach like the bitter taste of bile when he saw his horse point its ears and snort.

John petted the horse in an attempt to comfort him. He spoke to his horse in as calm a voice as he could muster. "Easy now, son." The horse's nostrils flared with the terrifying scent. He whinnied frantically as the horse reared and jerked the reins from John's hands. John could hear Slew Foot before he saw him. Small trees popped and snapped as the large grizzly plowed through the underbrush. An overwhelming panic overtook John. He ran as fast as he could in the direction of his fleeing horse. John felt Slew Foot getting closer, but he could not bring himself to look back. John foolishly dropped his rifle in hoping for greater speed. The fright had addled the mountain man's senses.

Most know that a bear could outrun a horse for a short distance. A man had no chance. A sweep of a massive paw broke one of John's legs. The trapper sprawled on his back, kicking at the grizzly with his one good leg. Slew Foot crunched John's head in its monstrous jaws. The giant bear loved the sound of a skull cracking open. The morsel of meat inside was a favorite. A normal grizzly does not announce a kill. Slew Foot was anything but normal. His roar silenced even the birds in the trees. With great relish, the grizzly ripped apart John's body as he thoroughly enjoyed the fulfilling flesh. Slew Foot mopped up the leftovers with his broad tongue.

Jack kissed Mountain Mist. "I'm going to gather up the old man and run our traps. I'll be back in a couple of days."

Mountain Mist stomped a foot. "Jack, you know I hate it when you're gone that long!"

Jack smiled. "I'll miss you too, but there are some things a man has got to do. Maybe I'll start taking you with me some."

Mountain Mist threw her arms around Jack, hugging his neck. "What about today? Take me today!"

Jack reluctantly pulled her arms down. "No, it won't be today. First, I got to get Kit used to the idea. I know he won't want a woman tagging along, even you."

Mountain Mist pouted as she rolled her eyes.

Two of Mountain Mist's best friends barged into her teepee after Jack was gone. Willow said excitedly, "I heard one of the warriors tell his wife that a plum thicket down by Red Creek was full of plums! Let's go quickly before they're all picked!"

Morning Dawn added, "Plums are my favorite! Come on, Mountain Mist, we don't want to be late!"

Mountain Mist could taste the sweet fruit in her imagination. She responded, "Let's go, but don't tell anyone we're going. Every Shoshone in the village will be down there."

The three women felt safe as Red Creek was only a few miles from the village. The Shoshone regularly traveled up and down the creek. It was also a place for relaxation. Young lovers would rendezvous under the shade of the trees. The cool breeze and the babble of the creek was the perfect spot for affairs of the heart.

Mountain Mist, Willow and Morning Dawn giggled and chattered as they plucked plums. Half of the succulent fruit made it into their baskets. The rest were eaten. The women laughed the most when they compared the pros and cons of their respective husbands. At one story Mountain Mist gagged, having to spit out the plum. That made the group laugh even louder. Their gaiety attracted the attention of an unwanted visitor. All three women froze at the unmistakable snuffle of a bear.

Slew Foot's pig-like eyes glistened at the sight of the three Shoshone. He clicked his teeth together one time before charging. Mountain Mist was the first to run. The mammoth grizzly sprang into the middle of the women. One chomp of his jaws broke the back of Willow. Slew Foot quickly pinned Morning Dawn and began tearing huge chunks of her flesh from her body. He briefly noted the flight of Mountain Mist before turning to the task at hand. Willow begged for mercy. She whimpered, "Please, please, please." The killing machine that was Slew Foot took no notice of Willow's cries. Instead, he ripped out her stomach, gulping it down in a feeding frenzy.

After eating Willow, Slew Foot took a break by slapping around the almost lifeless body of Morning Dawn. He was hopeful that he could encourage her to run so he could experience the thrill of chasing her down. When he didn't get the desired effect, the bear dismembered her, scattering body parts as far as fifty yards away. Slew Foot slated his considerable hunger by ambling to each limb. He left nothing but blood stains on the ground and trees.

Tears poured down Mountain Mist's face as she raced towards the village. She began screaming when the Shoshone camp came in sight. "Help me! Help me! It's coming!" Long Knife was the first to dash to meet her. He gathered his hysterical daughter in his arms. Mountain Mist kept twisting around, looking back in the direction from where she came.

Long Knife shook Mountain Mist as he spoke sternly, "Mountain Mist, you must calm down. I can't help you if I don't know what is wrong."

Mountain Mist struggled to catch her breath. Finally, she choked out, "A bear! It killed Willow and Morning Dawn!" With that, Mountain Mist became racked with sobs.

Long Knife turned his daughter over to the women of the village. He commanded half of his warriors to arm themselves and follow him. Long Knife told the others to stay and guard the people. It was an easy thing to backtrack Mountain Mist's trail. Even in a society where death was a daily part of life, it was hard to take in the scene where the women were killed by the grizzly.

The only thing left of Willow and Morning Dawn were a few bits of their deerskin dresses and a couple of bone splinters. The husband of Willow, Laughing Elk, dropped to his knees with the reality of the situation. Lone Badger who was married to Morning Dawn reached out to steady himself against a tree. None of the warriors spoke for several minutes. Long Knife broke the silence when he pointed at a huge track. "There… It can only be Slew Foot."

The worst suspicions of everyone were confirmed. The terror of the Wind River Mountains was in their territory. Long Knife drew a deep breath. "Come. We must go back to the village and make plans to hunt this bear. It fears no one. It will not leave on its on. We will have to kill it." The seriousness of the band of warriors climbed to a new height. Their way of life was being threatened. They could move the village, but the chances were good that the bear would only follow. Long Knife was wise enough to realize that either the bear would die or his people would.

Lone Badger surprised the Indians by shrieking a war whoop. He shouted, "I am a man! I will not go back to the village like a woman! This bear killed Morning Dawn! I was supposed to protect her! It must pay with its life!" Armed only with his bow and knife, Lone Badger started tracking Slew Foot.

Long Knife tried to stop him. "Lone Badger, it is foolish to go after this grizzly on your own. Come back with us. We will use the might of the Shoshone people to kill this bear."

Lone Badger waved him off, continuing to follow the wide trail of the killer grizzly. Lone Badger kicked his pace up to a trot. The tracks of Slew Foot were easy to follow. Within an hour, Lone Badger saw the monster bear. Slew Foot snarled when he saw the man coming his way. Lone Badger was running as he shouted a war cry. The warrior stopped when he got within range for his bow. He nocked an arrow, launching it into the center of Slew Foot's chest. Lone Badger screamed, "You killed my wife! Now it is your turn to die!" The grizzly snapped the shaft when he cuffed it with a paw. The sting of the arrow caused Slew Foot to bellow with rage. Lone Badger managed to get one more arrow into the bear before he was bowled over by the charge.

Slew Foot held down Lone Badger with one paw as he snarled with dripping fangs inches from the Shoshone's face. The foolish but brave warrior snarled back. The last thing Lone Badger saw was the gaping maw of the marauding grizzly. Slew Foot took extra satisfaction by devouring this challenge to its rule.

Long Knife left the village with twenty of his finest warriors. He decided to go on foot instead of horseback. The decision was guided by the chief's judgement that the ponies' response to the grizzly would not be manageable. Each of the Shoshone were grimly determined. That mood deepened when they discovered the remains of Lone Badger. Long Knife remarked after seeing how far the brave's blood was scattered and how torn up the ground was. "The bear was especially angry. We must be careful." The senses of sight and sound were at the maximum for the hunting Indians.

The only sound emitted by Slew Foot was a shallow panting as he watched the hunting party pass by his hidden location. Most of the Shoshone's focus was to the front and side. An attack from the rear seemed the least likely. Instinctively, Slew Foot began his charge in silence. Usually he loved to bellow his presence to put his prey in a state of panic. This time the huge grizzly killed two of the warriors with slicing swipes of his claws before the Indians could begin making adjustments to fight.

Three of the braves fled in panic without shooting an arrow. The rest stood their ground courageously as they nocked and shot. Arrow after arrow found their mark in the bear's hide. Each hit only made Slew Foot madder. Seeing the grizzly was systematically killing his men, Long Knife shouted to the four who remained, "This bear is a demon! It cannot be killed! Back to the village!"

Slew Foot was occupied with consuming thirteen dead Shoshone. He could not eat all the men in one feeding. The grizzly finished the next morning. He rolled around coating his fur in the remaining gore.

During the retreat to their camp, the three warriors who deserted the battle sheepishly joined in with what was left of the band. Long Knife offered no recriminations. He let the three fall in without comment. A mournful wail went up when the dispirited Indians entered the village. Long Knife had departed with twenty warriors, but returned with seven.

Mountain Mist rushed to her father. "You are hurt!" Her fingers gingerly felt of the deep claw marks on the chief's back. Mountain Mist choked up when she realized how close her father came to being killed.

When Jack began to pack his saddlebags to return to the Shoshone and Mountain Mist, Kit spoke up. "I see you're headed back to your woman. I think I'll ride along with you for a visit of my own. The older I get the less company my horse and the beaver pelts are. They used to be enough, but not no more."

Jack grinned. "Okay, but try not to get bullshit all over Long Knife. Remember, he's the chief."

Kit snorted. "Boy, don't think I can't take you down if need be. You might be young, but I got experience. Old beavers are harder to trap than young ones."

Jack replied, "I have to admit, you got me there."

Jack and Kit noticed the pall of sorrow that hung over the village. It was almost a real thing. Mountain Mist rushed up to Jack before he could even get down from his horse. She began crying. "Jack, it was awful. Willow and Morning Dawn are dead. That damn Slew Foot killed them both. Father went hunting for him with a band of our warriors. The bear killed most of them too!" Jack slid off his pony and wrapped his wife in his arms. Mountain Mist buried her face in the crook of his neck. Jack let her cry it out.

Kit went to Long Knife's teepee. Just as he got there, the chief came out. Kit clasped his arm in the Indian handshake. Kit asked, "What has happened, old friend?"

Long Knife slowly shook his head. "My people have committed some grave wrong. The Great Spirit has sent a demon to punish us."

Kit stroked his beard. "Let us smoke and talk this over. I know of no wrong by the Shoshone."

Mountain Mist begged her husband, "Jack, let's pack some things and go away. Just me and you! We will leave this bear far behind!"

Jack hugged her close again. "Listen to what you're saying. I know you're scared right now, but you couldn't leave your father or your people. You would always regret it."

Mountain Mist responded, "I am afraid, but not so much about me... I am afraid this demon-bear might kill you. I could not live if you are dead."

Jack smiled. "You forget, I'm not easy to kill. You could ask Scar, but he's no longer around. Besides that, old bear thinks of me as a friend. I did feed him once."

Mountain Mist frowned. "That is not funny. This bear killed my best friends and other members of the tribe who I have known all my life." After pausing, the Shoshone woman eyes flashed in anger. "I don't care if it's an evil spirit or not! I will end its life if it hurts you!"

Jack rubbed her shoulder and replied, "Let's eat. I'm hungry. I need to think about what needs to be done next."

Jack pulled his Hawken from the leather scabbard on his horse. He unsaddled it, stacking the saddle with his bow and arrows on top. Jack tied his powder horn and pouch of lead balls to a string of latigo, draping it over his shoulder.

Mountain Mist was nervous "What are you doing? Where are you going?"

Kit had just walked up behind him. Kit chimed in, "Yeah, that's a good question. Exactly where are you going?"

Jack shrugged. "I am Shoshone now. I must protect my people—"

Mountain Mist interrupted, "No! Please Jack!"

Jack gave his wife a brief hug.

Kit shook his head as he looked up in the sky in disbelief. "Boy, have you taken leave of your senses? You don't understand Slew Foot wiped out almost an entire war party? I'm not sure the U.S. Army could take down that damn bear and you're gonna try it all by your lonesome?" Kit paused. "Well, I'll tell you one damn thing. I'm going with you!"

Jack gave Kit a light slap on the back. "I appreciate the offer, but the fact that Slew Foot is so dangerous is the reason I've got to go alone. My only chance is to slip up on him without him knowing it. I don't think that two of us could do that. Maybe I can stick a musket ball in an ear before he knows I'm there."

Kit threw up his hands in disgust. He turned to Mountain Mist. "See if you can talk some sense into him. When the boy gets like this, there ain't much I can do with him."

Mountain Mist didn't say anything else. She knew it wouldn't do any good. Long Knife raised his hand to salute Jack as he left the village.

When Jack got to the site of the massacre, he was amazed at how much ground was torn up. Jack could picture in his mind's eye how the monstrous grizzly slaughtered and consumed the warriors. He could not hold back a small shudder. It took a day and a half to locate Slew Foot. Jack chewed on a couple of pieces of elk jerky to keep his hunger at bay.

Slew Foot was stalking along the edge of a cliff. His attention was on a spectacular waterfall that tumbled down the sheer face of the cliff. The grizzly stopped to lap up water from the stream that was the origin of the waterfall. Jack inched along the game trail towards the bear. Jack needed air in his lungs. He didn't realize that he had been holding his breath.

Jack slowly and deliberately brought up his rifle. He had a perfect angle for the ear shot he had hoped for. Just as he began to squeeze the trigger, Slew Foot jerked his head around. The grizzly's eyes bored into Jack's. In less than a second, Slew Foot started that deceptive loping gait that looked so slow, but was actually extremely fast. Jack knew he would have time for only one shot. A small cloud of smoke burst out of the muzzle. The musket ball cut through the smoke. Jack heard the thud of the ball striking the bear's head. Dust and blood flew from the impact.

Slew Foot slung his head, trying to get rid of the sting of the lead ball. The enraged bear slapped at everything that he came in contact with as he careened and rolled around. He lost sight of the edge of the cliff. A wrong step catapulted

Slew Foot off into thin air. The big grizzly cartwheeled end over end splashing into the river below. The thump of that huge body hitting the water caused beavers within a mile of the sound to whack their flat tails in response. Jack could not believe his good fortune as he watched the carcass of the terror of the north woods drift down the river until it was out of sight. Just before the remains of Slew Foot disappeared from view, Jack thought he detected a small movement. After giving it some thought, Jack decided the current from the river made it appear to move.

Mountain Mist had kept a vigil, sitting cross-legged as she watched the place where Jack had entered the woods in pursuit of the grizzly. Once, Kit came over. "You know, girl, that won't help him get back any sooner. Best thing for you is to go to your teepee and get some sleep." Mountain Mist didn't respond. She just shook her head. Kit muttered as he walked away, "Them two make a good pair. Both of them stubborn as hell."

The second Jack stepped from the woods, Mountain Mist sprang to her feet as she rushed to him. She screamed, "Jack!" just before launching herself into her husband's arms. The sheer force of Mountain Mist jumping on Jack dragged him to the ground. She lay on top of him, smothering him with kisses.

Jack kissed her back before laughingly saying, "Before going any farther, we probably should go to the teepee."

Mountain Mist laughed too as she pulled him to his feet and started towards the teepee. She didn't ask any questions. Mountain Mist was just happy to have her husband back.

By then the entire village had surrounded them as they trilled cries of joy. Kit interrupted their trip to the teepee.

"Now hold on there. You got plenty of time to be gallivanting. First, I want to know what happened? Did you find Slew Foot? You don't seem to be hurt so I reckon you didn't." The eager faces of the Indians suggested that they also wanted to know.

Jack grinned. "I found him. The last I saw of that ol' bear, his body was floating down the river." With that piece of news, the shouts of the Shoshone began again. This time it was much louder than before.

Long Knife interjected, "My people and me want to know how you killed him? Was he a spirit?"

Jack responded, "He wasn't no spirit. He was real enough. I managed to get a ball in his head. Slew Foot fell off a steep cliff into the river. I reckon he's gone for good." Everyone crowded around Jack congratulating him on his successful hunt. Jack just wished that tiny knot in his belly wasn't there.

Later Mountain Mist snuggled up to her husband under the warmth of the bear skins. She murmured, "I have some news."

Jack squirmed deeper in the skins. He was almost asleep. "What is your news?"

Mountain Mist kissed his neck. "You're going to be a father."

Jack squirmed a little more, settling into sleep. Suddenly he bolted upright. "What? What did you say?"

Mountain Mist softly laughed. "I said… you are going to be a father."

Jack was dazed. He sputtered, "Wh-ho... How did that happen?"

His wife smiled. "Jack, even a white man should know how it happened."

The American Fur Company finally sent out a replacement for George Atkins. Chester Ledbetter was as different from George as night is to day. Chester had been given the price parameters from the home office to negotiate for buying pelts. Instead of making the correct offer, Chester thought, *I would be loco to pay that much to these hillbillies. I'll carve myself out a small piece to help cover my expenses. No one will be the wiser.*

After meeting Chester, Kit walked out of the office with a funny look on his face. Most would not have noticed, but Jack did. Jack gave Kit a slight elbow. "Okay, what is it?"

Kit shrugged. "What is what?"

Jack retorted, "Don't give me that. The last time I saw that look is when that pouch of beaver urine broke, soaking your pants. You're looking the same way. Like you're smelling something sour."

Kit scrunched up his face. "It's just that... I dunno... That man makes my skin crawl. My gut says not to trust him."

Carl Baker hefted the small sack of gold dust in the palm of his hand. He remarked, "That's a little light, ain't it?"

Chester furrowed his forehead. "Times are hard. People ain't buying beavers for coats and hats like they used to. From what I hear, they've gone to buying something called chinchillas. Hell, they don't even have to trap them. Just raise 'em on a farm in Europe. When I heard that, I says to myself, 'Now, Chester, don't that beat all?' What will they think of next?" Chester could tell that Carl was still skeptical. He slapped the trapper on the back. "These things run in cycles. Next time you bring in a load of beaver, I might pay you twice what I'm paying now."

Chester had been a street hustler back in Boston. He became a notorious footpad, stealing anything that wasn't tied down. A couple of times he murdered someone to get their money. The Boston police finally viciously whipped him with their nightsticks. They dumped him on the edge of town. The sergeant warned him, "If we catch you back in Boston, you're going to get a one way trip to the boneyard. There won't be a nice funeral. Your body will rot where you lay."

Chester drifted west, going from town to town. Usually, he left a town with a police escort. When Chester landed in Kansas City, he became intrigued by the fur trade. Folks were talking about the fur business in the saloons and on the streets. Chester visited the local office of the American Fur Company. He was interested in finding out how he could get involved in the dealing of furs. Chester remembered the fine fur coats and hats back in Boston. As he sat in the outer sanctum, he heard the manager rail to his secretary in the back office, "Dammit! That's the third man this month who has turned me down for the Laramie job. People claim they want to work, but when I give them a chance, they come up with some lame excuse why they can't go. My pa always said that this generation don't know what it is to work."

As soon as the secretary came out, Chester asked, "Who do I need to see about a job?"

The woman replied, "You would need to speak to Mr. Johnson. He's our office manager... But maybe now would not be a good time. Can you come back some other day?"

Chester brushed by her.

She objected, "Sir! Sir! You can't go in there without an appointment!"

Chester burst through the office door. Before a startled Johnson could react, Chester blurted out, "I hear you need somebody to go to Laramie. I'm your man!"

Johnson dismissed the hovering secretary with a wave of his hand. Johnson stepped out from behind his desk. He looked Chester up and down. Johnson demanded, "What's your name?"

Chester answered, "Chester Ledbetter."

Johnson slowly circled before asking, "Got any experience in the fur business?"

Chester responded, "No, but how hard can it be? I figure I'd be buying hides. You tell me what you want and how much you'd be willing to pay. I'll take care of it. Simple."

Johnson sat back down at his desk. He continued, "You know how to ride a horse?"

Chester thought about all his escapes. "At a dead gallop, if need be."

Johnson strummed his fingers on his desk. He leaned forward, "Okay, here's the deal. You stay here for two weeks while I teach you how to judge pelts. You'll have to ride to Laramie. It's a long trip. I'm going to provide you a horse to ride and one to pack supplies. You don't show up at Laramie with my horses, I'll turn you in as a horse thief. I'll wire the bank that you're coming. They'll explain how to draw out money to pay for the hides. Most of the trappers don't have a use for paper money. They want to be paid in gold coins or gold dust. Your pay is two percent of each transaction. If you work hard, you can make a good living. I'm probably bat-shit crazy, but I'm going to take a chance on you."

With the price of beaver now set artificially low, the trappers weren't spending money in Laramie like they used to. The stores began to suffer.

Kent Fowler had a little run-in with the law back in Missouri. The sheriff had let him off with a warning. "Fowler, I've had about all of you I'm going to take. You're a pretty nice guy when you're sober. The problem is you ain't never sober. The next time you get drunk and start a fight, I'm gonna lock you up and throw the key down the well!" The sheriff turned to the woman, "Ma'am, you can take him home now. You heard what I said. Your man's about to go to living in jail."

Tessa replied, "Thank you, Sheriff. I appreciate you giving him another chance."

When they got back to the little shack they lived in, Tessa did something that she had never done before. She slapped the hell out of Kent. As he slowly got up from the floor, Kent rubbed the red mark on his face.

Kent exclaimed, "Have you lost your mind, woman? Nobody slaps Kent Fowler!"

Tessa retorted, "Shut up, Kent! Things are about to change around here. I'm getting ready to go out west for a fresh start. If you want to go with me, they'll be no more drinking! If you take a drink, I will change you from a rooster to a hen, muy pronto!"

Tessa decided that she wanted to open a dry goods store. She always loved shopping in dry goods stores when she was a child. She set up shop in a little rented building in Laramie. When she and Kent finished stocking, Tessa stepped back to admire it. "Well, Kent, that was a long trip by wagon train, but we made it. There were several times I thought we were done for. Somehow we're here and got our store."

Initially, things went well for the Fowlers. The merchandise in their store was in demand. Under the watchful eye of Tessa, Kent stayed off the rotgut. A change happened when the new agent for The American Fur Company started buying furs. The trappers' end became smaller and smaller. The trappers didn't have the money to spend at Fowler's Dry Goods.

One day, Chester Ledbetter paid a visit to Fowler's Dry Goods, but this time it wasn't to buy items unlike past visits. Chester made an offer. It was obvious Tessa was in charge. Chester addressed his remarks to her. "Mrs. Fowler, I know things have been rough lately with money being tight and all. Your store is important to Laramie. The town needs your store so I thought I'd just let you know that I have the funds to make you a loan if you ever need it."

Tessa blinked back tears. "That is so kind of you. Right now, we're going to try to scrape by. I hate the idea of going into debt, but I will certainly keep you in mind if it comes to that."

Chester tipped his hat. "If things get worse, let me know."

After Chester left the store, Tessa said to Kent, "Something just doesn't add up. Mr. Ledbetter knew we were hurting for money. He normally buys a nice bill of goods, but this time... nothing. That makes no sense."

Kent shrugged, as he wasn't paying attention to their finances. He was struggling with the growing desire to take a drink.

While running an errand, Chester saw Kent looking longingly at the Moose Head Saloon. Chester clapped Kent on the back. "Mr. Fowler, would you join me for a drink?"

Kent pulled back.

Chester laughed, "Sir, you look like you could use a drink. In fact, I'm buying!"

Kent checked for any sign of Tessa. He followed Chester. "Well, I guess one drink won't hurt nothing... 'specially since it's free." Kent didn't stop drinking until he was walking on his knees.

Chester helped him to his feet, then frowned. "It looks like I'm out of money. Why don't we go over to my office? I'll bet between the two of us, we can figure out a way to get more money. They ain't no reason to stop this party."

Kent grinned, bleary-eyed, "Nope! No reason at all!"

Chester quickly wrote out the agreement. He shoved the paper and a pen towards Kent. "Sign there, Mr. Fowler. You'll get that loan Mrs. Fowler wanted. And you'll have plenty of money for more whiskey. That way everybody gets what they want."

When Kent didn't come back on time after she sent him to buy fresh tomatoes, Tessa went looking for him. Dread welled up as she considered the Moose Head Saloon. Bracing herself for the worst, Tessa pushed through the batwing doors. Her fears were realized when she saw Kent passed out on a table in the corner. She jerked one of his ears, attempting to drag Kent off the table.

After the third jerk, Kent mumbled, "Oww." He partially sobered up when his eyes focused on his wife. Kent held up a leather pouch. "Look here, darling. I got you that loan you wanted."

After examining the gold coins in the pouch, Tessa retorted, "What is this? What loan, you drunken fool?"

Chester was leaned against the bar. He had decided to hang around to protect his investment. Chester responded, "Mrs. Fowler, it's so good to see you. Actually, that money is payment for your establishment. I tried to loan Kent the money, but he insisted on selling the store. I'm not a hard man like some. I will allow you three days to vacate my property. Be sure and leave the merchandise, as that was part of the sale too."

Kent tried to focus, "What?"

Chester showed Tessa the bill of sale. "You can see right there where Kent signed it."

Tessa counted the money twice to make sure the total was right. She pleaded, "Mr. Ledbetter, there must be some mistake. I did not want a loan. I certainly did not want to sell… Besides, this amount is only about half the value of my inventory!"

Chester shrugged. "I reckon Kent drank up the rest."

As Tessa started to leave the saloon with the pouch, Chester called after her, "Don't forget to take your husband with you!"

Tessa replied, "You can keep him. I don't want him."

After returning to the store she no longer owned, a despondent Tessa plopped down in the middle of the floor. She cocked the pistol and put the muzzle in her mouth. The bullet blowing off the top of her head assured that Kent was no longer her problem. No one knew exactly what happened to Kent. The day after Tessa was found, he was seen riding out of Laramie. His whereabouts after leaving was never known. Chester's only comment on viewing the scene of the suicide was, "Dammit! Look at the blood all over my goods! I bet most of it is ruined!"

Chester was rapidly becoming unpopular with the citizens of Laramie. Coupled with the diminishing prices for furs was an increase in prices for dry goods at Ledbetter Mercantile. Chester would wring his hands with false worry when faced with a complainant. "I just don't know how us working folks can survive much longer. I'm operating at a loss at the store, trying to help my friends." The truth was Chester was making more money than he had in his entire life.

Chester had become a regular at the Moose Head Saloon. Leland Carter was the owner. When the saloon came into existence, Leland was the barkeep for several years. Leland's wife and young son died suddenly from cholera. The saloon became like a family to him.

Leland prospered to the point that the saloon had rotating shifts of bartenders. Leland kept a table reserved for himself that no one else was allowed to occupy. Unlike Chester,

Leland was a well-liked figure in Laramie. It was known that if one was down on their luck, Leland could be counted on for a small loan. No one abused that policy because it was limited to a one-time access.

Because of his good nature, Leland welcomed Chester into his circle of friends. Chester swore his admiration of Leland. "I've got to hand it to you, Carter. You've built a helluva business here. If you're ever interested in selling the Moose Head, I'd like to buy it."

Leland laughed, "Sell the Moose Head? Not likely! What would I do every day? I would never consider that."

Chester would smile while nodding. "Can't say I blame you, but life is funny. Sometimes things change."

Chester wasn't satisfied skimming the American Fur Company or gouging the buyers at the mercantile. The more he got, the more he wanted. Greed became the driving force in his life. The thought had occurred to Chester that if he could acquire most of the businesses in town, he could live like a self-appointed king. Chester began imagining himself sitting on a throne with a crown of gold. People would bow down requesting his favor.

One night, after business had died down at the Moose Head, Leland stretched and yawned. "Well, boys, I reckon I'm gonna turn in for the night. There's always tomorrow to continue to bullshit each other." Everyone within earshot laughed.

After being home for about an hour, Leland heard a knock at the front door of his house. Leland had already dropped off to sleep but got up to answer the knock that was steadily increasing in volume. "All right! All right! I'm coming!"

When he swung open the door, Leland was surprised. "Chester, what are you doing here? Do you know what time it is?"

Chester grinned. "Sorry about the lateness of calling on you, but there's something that won't wait until tomorrow."

The affable Leland stepped off to one side. "Come in. I'll make us a pot of coffee."

Chester replied, "That would be just fine. I appreciate it."

Both men sat down at the kitchen table with steaming cups of coffee. In response to Leland's questioning look, Chester began, "See here, Leland, I've mentioned to you several times about buying the saloon. The time for talk is over. We need to get on with it—"

Leland interrupted, "Chester, what the hell are you talking about? How many times do I have to tell you that I ain't interested in selling. I can't believe you woke me up in the middle of the night for this. You need to leave!"

Chester smiled. "I will leave as soon as you sign this bill of sale transferring the Moose Head to me." Chester reached under his coat then slid the document across the table.

Leland jumped up, pointing a finger towards the door. "Get out!"

Chester pulled a pistol out from his coat. "Sit back down or I'll blow a hole in you that you could throw a whiskey bottle through."

As he slowly sank back down in his seat, Leland murmured, "You're plumb loco."

Chester went on like he wasn't holding a gun on the saloon owner. "Now, see here. This is where you sign. Don't worry. I'm gonna pay you a fair price. We'll go over to my office and I'll get you the money."

Through his amazement, Leland asked, "And if I don't sign?"

Chester shrugged. "Then you don't give me no choice but to scatter your brains all over this nice kitchen."

After Leland reluctantly scribbled his signature, he threw down the pen. "Ledbetter, this will never hold up in court. I'll testify that I signed because there was a gun to my head!"

Chester carefully folded the bill of sale, sticking it back in his coat. The new owner of the Moose Head Saloon sighed. "I was afraid you might say that." Chester triggered the pistol. The ball smashed through Leland's right eye. When it exited the back of his skull, the kitchen was splattered with red blood, gray brain matter and white chips of bone.

Chester was the first customer in the saloon after the bartender unlocked the door the next morning. The barkeep grinned. "You getting kinda of an early start today, aren't you, Mr. Ledbetter?"

Chester's only response was, "Whiskey."

In about an hour there was an uproar out in the street. Someone dashed through the batwings. "Leland Carter's been found murdered! Someone blew his brains out!" The bartender poured himself a shot of whiskey and sat down at Chester's table. After downing his drink, he stared at the empty glass. "What is the world coming to? A man can't count on anything these days." The bartender looked up at

Chester. "What do you suppose will happen to Leland's saloon?"

Chester responded, "He don't own the Moose Head no more. I do. I bought it last night."

The city fathers had recently elected young Ralph Cramer as the town's first sheriff. While Ralph had never worked in law enforcement, Mayor Young endorsed the move. "Look, I know Ralph is green, but he's a good boy. The kid is smart. He'll learn. Besides we can always fall back on Major Henderson and the soldiers if things get too rough for Ralph." What went unsaid was that Ralph would work cheap. Cost was a big factor with the taxpayers of Laramie.

Shortly after word got out that Chester Ledbetter was the new owner of the saloon, Sheriff Cramer paid Chester a visit, backed by a contingent of concerned citizens headed by Mayor Young. The new sheriff tipped his hat. "Good day, Mr. Ledbetter. It's come to my attention that Leland Carter supposedly sold you this saloon the night he was murdered. That's kind of a big coincidence, don't you think? I'm afraid I'm going to have to see the bill of sale."

Chester retorted, "There ain't no 'supposedly' about it. He sold me the Moose Head. And I can prove it." Chester smoothed out the document on the table.

Cramer read and examined the bill of sale. When he handed it back to Chester, the sheriff remarked, "Well, I ain't no lawyer, but everything looks nice and legal."

Mayor Young stepped around the young sheriff and snatched the bill of sale from Chester's hands. "Let me see that! There ain't no way Leland would have sold the Moose Head. He told me he planned on dying on one of the tables when his time came." Mayor Young continued, "That's his signature, all right, but something just ain't right." Young addressed Chester, "It's a mighty big coincidence that Leland Carter, who I've known for twenty years, just up and decided to sell. Then in the next breath, somebody puts a ball through his head. I think you're guilty as hell of murdering my friend. If it's the last thing I do, I'm going to prove it."

Chester gave a half-smile. "Got any witnesses?"

At first, business fell off at the saloon. Folks stayed away as a way showing respect for Leland, a town favorite. But eventually, the lure of alcohol proved to be too much. Within a week, men were clamoring for a drink. Surveying the crowd, Chester smirked, "So much for friendship!"

Realizing how unpopular he was, plus making money hand over fist, Chester decided to hire a couple of bodyguards to watch his back.

Blackjack Cooper was a card cheat and a master of the hide-out gun. He asked permission of Chester. "Mr. Ledbetter, I'm Blackjack Cooper. The one thing your saloon is missing is a poker game. I can provide that game. Your cut will be twenty-five percent of the net for letting me operate out of the Moose Head."

Chester strummed his fingers on the table before asking, "How do I know that there is going to be a 'net'?"

Blackjack grinned. "'Cause I'm one of the best. Besides, I ain't asking for no money, just a place to run my game."

Chester paused. He liked the idea of making more money, but something didn't add up. Chester continued, "Mr. Cooper, if you're a good as you say you are, why are you here in this godforsaken country? There ain't many bright lights in these parts. I would think a gambler—especially a successful one—would live in a city with fine hotels and fine restaurants."

Blackjack's face reddened. "Well, that's a good question… You see, I had me a run-in with a sheriff that had it in for me. There was just no pleasing him. I eventually left town. That kind of stuff keeps happening to me, so I decided to try a place where a man can make his own laws. That's why I come out here."

Chester smirked. "Sorry, that don't make no sense either. That's too thin. We got a sheriff plus a whole garrison of soldiers at the fort. Why do think you can make your own laws?"

Blackjack's body sagged as if all the air had been let out. He dejectedly responded, "All right, I guess it's been more than one town that's posted me… But there ain't no risk to you. At least give it a chance."

In the end, Chester agreed to let Blackjack have his chance. Initially, everything went as Blackjack projected. In fact, Chester's end kept getting larger and larger. Blackjack laid down cash on Chester's table. "Here ya go, boss. Just like I said. I'm making you money."

Chester retorted after counting the money, "I reckon you were right, but let's see if you can keep it up."

The cowboy swore, "I seen that, you sum bitch! That last card came off the bottom of the deck!" As the cowboy went for his six-shooter, Blackjack activated the spring-loaded derringer that was up his sleeve. Both men fired at the same time. The bullet from the derringer crashed through the cowboy's nose, penetrating his brain. He died instantly. The slug from the six-shooter blew off three fingers on Blackjack's right hand.

The cowboy's body slumped over the table. Blackjack yelled in pain as he grabbed his hand. The bartender managed to stop the bleeding while somebody went to get the doctor. The doctor finished bandaging Blackjack's hand as he remarked, "Mister, I guess you're going to have to find you a new line of work. You won't be dealing any more cards with that hand."

The smile almost split apart the adopted Shoshone's face as Jack held up the bawling baby. Jack laughed at the squirming boy. He exclaimed, "Now aren't you the little bobcat?" Jack laughed harder as the baby continued raising a ruckus. He handed the boy back to Mountain Mist. "Since he's my son, I suspect he's hungry." Mountain Mist nestled the baby to her breast. At the sight of the baby greedily grabbing and sucking his mother's nipple, Jack laughed again. "Yep, that's my boy all right!"

Kit showed up unexpectedly the day the baby was born. Jack asked with a grin, "Why ain't you out tending our traps?" Jack suspected Kit got lonesome again. This was a new emotion for Kit. All those years he trapped by himself, he never had anyone to miss. Now he had Jack.

Kit responded, "Don't you worry about it none. I got it under control." Kit heard the baby crying. "The young'un's here?"

Kit laughed. "Let me go get him… that is if I can get him off his mother's teat long enough."

Kit muttered, "Just like his pa."

Kit laughed as he held the squalling baby up in the bright sunlight. "I can tell right now. This one will be good to ride the river with. Have you thought of a name for the little rascal?"

Jack responded, "Mountain Mist and me were talking about just that thing. We thought we might call him… Kit Bear."

Kit quickly handed the baby back to Jack, rapidly walking away. He didn't want Jack to see the tears welling up in his eyes. Jack did hear him say, "Dammit, boy."

Later, Kit asked Jack, "Are you sure you and Mountain Mist want to brand him with that name?"

Jack smiled. "We're sure."

Later that night, Jack and Kit were smoking with Long Knife. Kit exhaled as he passed the pipe. "We sure got us a mess up in Laramie."

Jack frowned. "Now what?"

Kit replied, "It's that damn American Fur Company. I guess they don't make em like ol' George anymore. This new agent they sent us is a rattlesnake without the rattles. I think he's short stroking everybody on the fur prices and if that ain't enough, he claims he bought the Moose Head from Leland Carter."

Jack responded, "Well, what does Leland say?"

Kit exploded, "He don't say shit! It's hard to talk when you had your brains blowed out!"

The men continued smoking for a while. Finally, Jack said, "Maybe we ought to mosey on up to Laramie and get the lay of the land."

Kit replied, "You can get the lay of the land all you want, but they weren't no witnesses. That coyote needs a dose of mountain justice."

Jack stroked his beard. "We can do whatever needs done."

Kit responded, "You stay and look after Mountain Mist and young Kit Bear. I'll ride up there. If I need you, I'll send for you."

A week later, Jack returned to the trappers' camp. He was surprised to see Jerimiah Jenkins warming his hands at a fire. Jerimiah answered Jack's unasked question. "I figured you'd be around directly. I don't cotton to riding into no Injun camp even though I knowed you was friendly with them, having married one and all... It's Kit. He's been shot. It's pretty bad. Kit's a rough ol' cob, but he may not make it."

The only soft spot in Chester's heart was for money. It wasn't out of generosity that he offered Blackjack a job. "That was a tough break. It's gonna be hard for a cripple to find work. As far as I know, the only thing you know how to do is deal cards."

A dejected Blackjack agreed. "I reckon you're right. I thought for a spell that I might learn to deal left-handed." Blackjack sighed deeply. "I tried it and it didn't work."

Chester responded, "The way I see it, you only got two options: begging on the street, which folks ain't going to put with, or you can come to work for me. Times are hard so I can't pay much, but at least you can eat and have a place out of the rain."

Blackjack brightened. "If I worked for you, what would I have to do?"

Chester's eyes narrowed. "Whatever I tell you with no sniveling!"

Kit came through the batwing doors with something on his mind. He strode over to Chester's table and leaned in so his face was a foot from Chester's. "I was a friend of Leland Carter. I knowed you kilt him. Hell, everybody knows you kilt him! The rest of them are too hung up in doing things all nice and legal. I ain't worried about going by the law. Mountain justice is more important to me. I'm just the man who can see you get what you got coming to you!" Kit stomped out the door.

The next day a voice called out to Kit from a darkened alley. "Mr. Bridger! Mr. Bridger! I got a message from Jack. He told me to be sure nobody sees me give it to you." Mentioning Jack's name took the edge off Kit's caution. Without thinking it through, Kit stepped into the alley. Two blasts from a pistol greeted him. One bullet struck him high in the chest, the other low in the belly. Blackjack turned and ran, fleeing the scene of the shooting.

A passerby heard the shots. He entered the alley, discovering Kit's bleeding body. He exclaimed, "As I live and breathe, it's Kit Bridger!"

Jack knocked on the door of the doctor's office. Doc opened it, motioning Jack to come in. The doctor could tell that Jack was worried. Jack asked, "How is he?"

Doc replied, "I'll be honest. When I first got him, I didn't think he would make it through the night. But that was three days ago. Kit is a stubborn cuss that these mountains seem to breed. He's a little better, but not out of the woods yet. A normal man I would give a fifty-fifty chance of survival. A mountain man like him will probably make it."

Jack breathed a sigh of relief. "Can I see him, Doc?"

Doc nodded. "Go ahead. He's in the next room. It will probably do him good."

Jack slowly pushed open the door. If Kit was sleeping, he didn't want to wake him up. Kit greeted Jack with a scowl. "It's about time you dragged your carcass up here! I was dying, you know!"

Jack grinned. He was now confident Kit would recover. Jack protested, "What did you expect me to do? Somebody had to work our traps. It obviously wasn't going to be you. You were too busy lying in this soft bed!"

Kit busted out laughing. Jack joined him, carefully giving Kit a hug.

Jack sat in a chair next to the bed. His countenance changed from joy to a more somber mood. "Who did this?"

Kit responded, "I didn't get a good look at his face. I did see he was holding his pistol with two hands. One of the hands had several fingers missing. I reckon if we could find that hand with the fingers gone, we'd have our man. Hold on. Let me get my britches on and we'll go look."

Jack held up one hand. "Hold on yourself. You ain't getting out of bed. I got work to do. I can't do it nursemaiding you."

Kit raised up an inch before collapsing back on the bed. He breathed heavily. "I reckon I may need another hour or two."

Jack squeezed Kit's hand. "You take it easy, oldtimer. There's a reason you got a partner. Let me do my job."

The first person Jack asked about someone missing fingers, replied, "There's that four-flushing dealer who works for Ledbetter over at the Moose Head Saloon. At least he used to be a card dealer until he was caught cheating. A cowboy blew off most of his fingers on one hand."

Armed with that information, Jack headed for the saloon. He ordered a beer, sipping it slowly as he leaned up against the bar. A man walked by. Jack seized his wrist in an iron grip, twisting it in such a way that the man was forced to his knees. Jack demanded, "How'd you lose these fingers, friend?"

Blackjack squealed, "Oouuhh! That hurts! Let me go!"

Jack twisted his wrist harder. "Answer the damn question!"

Blackjack begged, "Please, mister! I ain't never done nothing to you!"

Jack applied more pressure. "If you don't talk, I'm gonna snap your hand off and feed it to the wolves!"

Blackjack began sobbing as he slumped to the floor. "I'll tell you whatever you want... just let me go."

Jack kept twisting Blackjack's wrist. The onlookers swore they could hear the bones in his wrist begin to pop.

Blackjack managed to squeak out, "Some crazy cowboy shot em off!"

Jack continued, "That ain't all I want to know. Why did you shoot Kit Bridger?"

Blackjack cried. "I don't know what you're talking about!"

Jack finished snapping off Blackjack's hand at the wrist. The bones were sticking through the skin. Blackjack screamed as he bawled like a baby.

Jack dropped the limp wrist and grabbed the other one. Jack grinned. "We got us a fresh one to work with." The mountain man pulled his skinning knife. "We're going to do this new hand a little different. I'm going to cut off these fingers until you tell me what I want to know."

Blackjack blubbered, "Please stop!"

Jack sliced off the little finger, prompting the killer to screech even more. Jack responded, "You're taking too damn long to answer my questions! Do it faster or you're going to end up eating with your elbows!"

Blackjack pleaded, "I'll tell you whatever you want to know!"

Jack smiled, "That's better. Now, why did you shoot Kit?"

Blackjack said haltingly, "I was paid to shoot him."

Jack nodded. "Now we're getting somewhere. Who paid you?"

Blackjack choked out, "It was Ledbetter… Chester Ledbetter."

Every face in the saloon turned towards Chester's table. He had vanished, slipping out the back when he saw things weren't going his way. In one quick motion, Jack almost severed Blackjack's head with a slash of his knife. His head flopped to one side similar to his hand. Blood gushed from the wound as it drenched the floor red. Jack looked up at the shocked faces. He said matter-of-factly, "The sum bitch shouldn't have shot my friend."

Chester was in a panic. He was at his office at the American Fur Company. Chester was throwing cash, gold coins and gold dust into a set of saddlebags. As he emptied his safe, a voice from the darkness asked, "Going somewhere?"

Chester whirled around, almost falling down. When the apparition that was Jack Flint materialized in the light, Chester stammered, "T-th… That damn Blackjack is a liar! I didn't have nothing to do with the shooting of Bridger!" Jack's expressionless face seemed to be chiseled in stone. Chester shouted, "Look here! I got money! You can have half!" When Jack didn't respond, Chester added, "Okay, all! You can have it all! I'll leave town! You won't ever see me again!"

The tears that can only come when someone is facing their own death began to flow down Chester's cheeks. Chester whimpered as he stared down the muzzle of the big Hawken. The ball exploded the thief's skull. Bits and pieces of Chester Ledbetter were scattered around the room.

Jack sat down in the chair next to Kit's bed. Kit opened his eyes. "What are you doing back so soon? Decided you needed my help after all, didn't you? Boy, you need to listen better."

Jack smiled as he tossed the two objects on the bed. When Kit focused on them, he shrank back in revulsion. "Boy, have you taken leave of your senses? Get them bloody things off my bed. What are they anyway?"

Jack replied, "The finger is from the one who shot you. The scalp is from the one who hired him."

Kit swore, "Sum bitch!"

When Sheriff Cramer asked about the deaths of Chester and Blackjack, Mayor Young responded, "Let it go, Sheriff. You don't hear anybody squawking, do you? That's 'cause mountain justice was served. Them two got what they deserved."

Major Henderson decided to conduct his own investigation. After the third person he questioned said they didn't know anything, Henderson threw up his hands in frustration. "Back to the fort, men. It appears that the good folks of Laramie are satisfied with two men being murdered in broad daylight."

The legend of Jack Flint continued to grow. More than one mountain man was heard to mutter, "That ol' boy still has the bark on."

Snake Eye heard of the exploits of Jack. Like his father, Scar, the blood raged hotly in Snake Eye's veins with jealousy. He was still reluctant to lead an open attack on the Shoshone camp. The Crow chieftain wasn't willing to sacrifice his warriors unless victory was assured. That all changed the day Snake Eye found out that Jack had married a Shoshone woman and they had a baby. The opportunity to kill the white man was worth all his warriors. A plan began to form.

That night around the roaring campfire, Snake Eye made his scheme known to attack the Shoshone village. He announced, "The Great Spirit has given me direction for my people. I will lead a war party against the Shoshone. We will wipe them from the earth!" The young men began to scream war cries and threats as they danced in a frenzy. The older men were more reserved with doubt about the wisdom of this raid. In the end, no one challenged their chief. Most knew that to do so would be certain death.

After the raid of the grizzly, Long Knife started posting nightly guards around the village. In the dim light of the predawn, three arrows thumped into the hearts of the three guards. Crow warriors quickly closed the distance to the Shoshone, slashing their throats to eliminate any additional noise. One of the camp dogs heard a slight rustle of leaves. When he went to investigate, he yelped as an arrow cut short his life.

The village was beginning to stir with people gathering firewood, water and relieving themselves. The crisp mountain air was suddenly filled with whistling arrows as everyone who were exposed were cut down. War whoops were shrieked as the Crow warriors rushed to attack. The Shoshone spilled out of their teepees eager to meet their old enemies in combat. Surprise was with the marauders. Several of the Shoshone gave as good as they got.

Big Horn fought back-to-back with his wife, Kicking Squaw. They both howled in horror as their two young children were slaughtered before their eyes. Kicking Squaw screamed, "Little Horn, my son!" She slashed at the Crows to no avail. There were just too many of them. As she succumbed to her many stab wounds, her last sight was her daughter's scalp hanging from a Crow lance. Big Horn killed four of the invading Crows before falling with more than a dozen arrows sticking from his body.

Snake Eye screeched, "Stop! That is their chief. He is mine!" The surrounding Crows took a step back away from Long Knife. The Shoshone chief was shielding Mountain Mist and Kit Bear, sweeping the air with his blade. Mountain Mist bared her teeth and growled. They would only get her child after she was dead.

Snake Eye confronted Long Knife. The Crow discarded his bow and arrow, leaving him with just a knife as he mirrored the Shoshone. Snake Eye cackled, "I hear you are a great warrior! No one is as great as me! Not even my father, Scar! You are a disgrace to your tribe allowing your daughter to marry a white man. I will restore her dignity by making her one of my wives. Her whelp by the white man will grow up a slave to my people."

Long Knife had built a reputation as a knife fighter down through the years. His advancing age had slowed him down. Long Knife no longer had the rattlesnake speed to utilize against an opponent. The Shoshone chief threatened, "You will not have my daughter or my grandson. I will cut your Crow hide into many pieces. The worms will feast on you!"

Snake Eye smirked. "You have gotten old. I could have beaten you even in your youth. You cannot win. Accept your fate and I will kill you quickly."

Long Knife responded to the Crow's warning by a thrust of his knife that took a chunk out of Snake Eye's arm. The sight of his own blood infuriated Snake Eye. He stooped, grabbing a handful of dirt. The Crow slung the dirt into Long Knife's face, temporarily blinding him. Snake Eye rapidly began stabbing the defenseless Shoshone. Long Knife staggered to his knees with his chest and legs covered in blood.

Snake Eye screamed his war cry as he jerked up Long Knife's hair. The Crow sliced a portion of Long Knife's scalp away from the Shoshone's skull while he was still alive. Snake Eye danced with the bloody scalp raised high.

Mountain Mist shouted, "Father!" as she tried to go to his aid. Two of the Crow warriors grabbed her arms. A third one snatched Kit Bear away from her. Mountain Mist was powerless. She could do nothing about Long Knife or Kit Bear. Mountain Mist watched her father die and her son carried off. Her final thought before Snake Eye knocked her unconscious for trying to help her family, was, *My husband will come for us. I will see my people revenged when Jack gets here.*

Snake Eye's last act before leading the triumphant return to the Crow encampment was to order his men, "Burn it!"

There were some survivors from the Crow massacre. Four Shoshone warriors were gone on a hunting party. Six women with three of their children had managed to slip away during the chaos of the battle. Snake Eye didn't look hard for them. He wanted some to live to tell of his great victory.

When the warriors and women returned, they wailed bitterly for the many killed. The camp was littered with bodies. The Shoshone were further upset because the Crow had looted the village. There were no skins to wrap the bodies for burial. Instead, they began the arduous task of dragging the dead to a deep crevice. Pushing them over the edge was the only option the Shoshone had. It was better than leaving their loved ones to be scavenged by wolves.

During this process, the oldest warrior said to the youngest, "You must find Jack Flint. Tell him all that has happened."

Jack cocked his head at the sound of a rapidly approaching horse. The breathless Shoshone slid his pony to a stop and leapt off. He declared, "Jack Flint, it is the Crow. They attacked our village. Many have died."

A horror-stricken Jack interrupted, "Mountain Mist and my boy! Are they dead?"

The young brave shook his head. "They live but they have been carried off by the Crow."

Jack asked, "Long Knife?"

The Shoshone dropped his head. "It appears he fought like the great chief he was."

Jack had heard enough. He sprang on his horse, immediately heeling it into a gallop. Jack didn't bother to find and notify Kit. He knew they old mountain man would piece together what had happened. Kit would be along directly.

Upon his arrival at what was left of the Shoshone village, Jack did not take the time to dismount. He told one of the men, "I cannot help you. I must find Mountain Mist and my child." The Shoshone nodded his agreement. The returning war party made a wide path. There was no concern that anyone would be foolish enough to follow them.

When Jack had tied his horse at a distance, he snuck up on the Crow village. The entire tribe was engaged in a raucous celebration over the annihilation of their hated enemies. Snake Eye had tied Mountain Mist to a post in the middle of the camp. He had given Kit Bear to a woman who still had milk remaining from her baby who had recently died. Snake Eye told her, "Take care of this whelp. He will serve our tribe for many years." No one noticed that the Crow chieftain kept secretly cutting his eyes around the horizon. He was waiting on Jack. Snake Eye was counting on Jack showing up. The white man's death would complete the victory over the Shoshone. It would further enhance Snake Eye's reputation with his people. Their songs would say that he was a greater warrior than Scar.

Jack took it all in. He was relieved that Mountain Mist and Kit Bear were still alive. Jack settled in the concealing thicket. He would wait until the time was right.

Jack smiled at the conditions. The sky was overcast, blocking out any light from the moon and stars. It was so dark that one couldn't see their hand held up inches from their face. Jack's uncanny eyesight allowed him to see while his enemies were practically blind.

Jack had made a mental note of each teepee location. Mountain Mist was still tied to the post but was slumped over in an exhausted sleep. Jack removed his boots. Bare feet contributed to a silent approach. The Crow were in a deep sleep themselves, weary from their extensive celebration.

Some of the teepees Jack entered through the tent flap. Others entry was made through a small slit from Jack's knife in the side. The outcome was the same. Jacks cut open the throats of everyone in the teepee—man, woman and child.

After killing the inhabitants of about half of the teepees, Jack realized he was running out of time. He closed his hand around Mountain Mist's mouth. He didn't need to say anything. She knew it was him. After cutting the ropes that bound her, he pulled her hand to follow him. Mountain Mist knew where Jack was leading her. When they got to the teepee that contained Kit Bear, Mountain Mist squeezed Jack's arm. She took the knife from him. The wet nurse was the only one in the teepee with Kit Bear. As Mountain Mist dragged the edge of the blade, opening the woman's throat, she whispered in the Crow's ear, "You can't have him." Mountain Mist punctuated her contempt by stabbing the wet nurse twice in the heart.

Somehow even as a tiny baby, Kit Bear knew to be quiet as he was carried from the Crow village to safety. Mountain Mist rode behind Jack as she cradled Kit Bear. After going a considerable distance, Mountain Mist murmured, "I knew you'd come."

Jack reached back, stroking her leg. He said quietly as they rode, "I am sorry about Long Knife and your people. Long Knife was a great man."

Mountain Mist had already stoically accepted the deaths. She responded, "It is hard to believe that my people are no more."

Jack replied, "They are not all dead. Thirteen survived. Enough to build back the Shoshone tribe."

When they arrived at the remnant of the Shoshone camp, Kit was there waiting on them. He rushed over, helping Mountain Mist and the baby down. Kit blinked back tears. "I will miss Long Knife. He was a helluva man. I'm damn proud to have knowed him!"

Mountain Mist put her hand on Kit's arm, "He thought so much of you, Kit. Initially, there was a concern among some about his friendship with you. Father didn't care. He felt you were special."

Kit ducked his head. "Stop it, girl. You're gonna get me to blubberin'." The old mountain man reached over to pat Kit Bear. "How is the young'un? If anybody hurt that boy, they're gonna have to deal with me."

Mountain Mist smiled. "Kit Bear is fine."

Kit always grinned at the baby's name.

Jack had never gotten off his horse. He spoke, "Kit, you see after them. I've got some business to take care of."

Kit responded, "Don't you worry none. No sum bitch will touch 'em while I'm around!"

Jack heeled his horse into a trot as he headed back in the direction of the Crow camp.

The Crow village woke up at dawn to an unspeakable horror. The shrieking rose to a crescendo as teepee after teepee was discovered with bodies lying in pools of blood. The red blood looked black in the shadows of the teepees. The Crow left alive began to hastily strike their teepees to move to a different location.

Snake Eye was furious. "What are you doing? I gave no orders to take down the teepees! You must stop!"

One of the elders answered, "This ground is cursed by the Great Spirit. He sent a demon among us to kill our people. We will not stay here."

Snake Eye jerked his knife from his scabbard. "I will kill anyone who attempts to leave!"

To the chief's shock and surprise, the rest of the remaining warriors brandished their weapons in opposition to Snake Eye. Seeing that he could no longer rule by intimidation, Snake Eye spat in contempt, "You will die without me leading you! No one is as fierce in battle as me! No one is as wise as me!"

The rest of the Crow seemed to be content to move on without their former chief.

As Snake Eye watched the rest of the Crow disappear from sight, he vowed, "It was no demon! It was that white man! I will find him and kill him. Before he dies, he will see me take his woman and scalp his child." Snake Eye leapt on his pony and started for the Shoshone village.

Jack was not in a hurry. He knew that the Crow were not going anywhere, but if they did, they would be easy to track. Jack periodically whoaed his pony as he looked and listened. He was intent on killing Snake Eye for what the Crow had tried to do to his family, but realized caution was important. As he sat in a small grove of aspens, the birds and the normal sounds of the forest went silent.

Snake Eye was picking his way along the trail. The anger still raged in him toward the white man. He thought, *When I am finished with Jack Flint, I will find my people. I will kill the traitors among them.* Engrossed in thought, the Crow did not realized Jack was there until an Apache war cry rang out. Before Snake Eye could respond, he and his horse were rammed from the side by Jack's pony. The force of the collision tossed Snake Eye against a tree. His head struck the trunk, knocking him unconscious.

When Snake Eye groggily regained consciousness, he tried to rise to his feet. It took a moment for him to realize that he was staked out. His arms and legs were immobilized by stout leather cords anchored by secure stakes. The former Crow chief thrashed violently when he saw Jack standing over him.

Jack laughed at his struggles. "I killed your father and I will kill you. You will beg me for death. You put your hands on my wife and child. That will cost you your life."

Jack squatted by a small fire. He heated his knife blade by turning it over and over in the flame. Snake Eye gave up any semblance of courage when Jack peeled of the first inch of skin on his inner thigh. The scream intensified as Jack cauterized the wound with the hot blade of his knife. It took Jack three days and nights to finish skinning Snake Eye. Despite Snake Eye pleading and begging, "Kill me! Please kill me!" Jack continued his grim task. Mountain justice demanded it.

The last of the Shoshone Nation, including his family, greeted Jack when he returned to camp. When Jack related the news of the death of Snake Eye, joyous whoops echoed through the mountains. Even Kit cocked back his head and howled like a wolf. Everyone dissolved in laughter when little Kit Bear was fascinated and tried to mimic his namesake. Kit Bear's howl was a kitten's mew.

That night over the communal campfire, the oldest member of the tribe presented Long Knife's smoking pipe to Jack. He had found it while going through the rubble. The elder Shoshone spoke. "This is more than a gift, Jack Flint. You should be the new chief of the Shoshone."

Jack stammered, "Th-that's a great honor, but don't you think your new chief should be a Shoshone?"

The elder replied, "You have proven yourself worthy to be Shoshone."

Jack looked at Mountain Mist. She nodded her head in approval. Jack turned to Kit, "How do you feel about this?"

Kit shrugged. "It makes sense to me. We can still run our traplines, but instead of having to continually move our camp, we can live here with our Indian friends."

Jack looked upward, viewing the twinkling stars in the night sky. When he felt a confirming acceptance, Jack received the pipe. "I am proud to be the chief of the Shoshone."

Jack prepared to ride off the next morning. "I need to see what happened to the Crow. I want to make sure we are no longer vulnerable to their raids." He nodded to Kit. "Take care of my family." Jack followed the trail of the fleeing Crow for almost a hundred miles. When it was apparent that the Crow were leaving the mountains, Jack wheeled his pony to return to the Shoshone village.

Sanchez, the leader of a notorious band of Comancheros was told by a scout whose job was to gather information for future raids. "I hear the Crow almost wiped out the Shoshone up at Wind River. There's enough of them left to make a little trip worthwhile. We can sell their scalps down in Mexico. The Federales are paying many pesos for Indian hair. They want Comanche or Apache, but how the hell would they know the scalps were Shoshone?"

Sanchez was captured by the Comanche when he was four years old during a raid in Mexico. The Comanche ravaged his small village. All the Mexican men and women were put under the knife or were burned alive. The women were used every way a man can use a women before they were killed. Sanchez was an eyewitness to the slaughter of his father and mother. The leader of the Comanche commanded, "Take the boy with us. The Comancheros pay well for slaves." The Comanche had no idea what were the names of the boy or his family. He named him Sanchez because that was the name of the half-breed who commanded the Comanchero band.

The bandit chief laughed. "So the boy is named Sanchez like me?"

The Comanche solemnly nodded. "Yes, that is why I brought him to you. I thought he might be a member of your family."

Sanchez laughed again. "I don't think you know his name… but it doesn't matter. I will give you two bottles of tequila for him."

The Comanche quickly agreed. He loved drinking tequila better than laying with a woman. At least with the liquor, he didn't have to hear it whine that he was hurting it.

Sanchez spun the boy around. He grinned, showing his gold teeth. "You are a fine looking chico!" Then Sanchez back-handed the boy so hard that he left his feet, flying through the air. The boy began to cry when he landed with a thud on the hard ground. Sanchez grabbed the front of kid's raggedy shirt. He shook the boy, making his teeth rattle. Sanchez smiled. "This is to let you know you should fear me. Do as I say every time I tell you and you will live. Disobey me and you will die!" Sanchez began referring to the boy as

Little Sanchez. As Little Sanchez grew up, he suffered many beatings at the hands of the bandit leader.

As with most Comancheros at that time, Sanchez and his gang members practiced every form of perversion. He demanded that Little Sanchez begin drinking tequila at the age of eight. Over the years, that abuse of alcohol impaired Little Sanchez's brain. When the boy turned ten, Sanchez demanded that Little Sanchez use a woman. He cackled, "It's time you become a man." He ordered the Mexican whore, "Teach the boy. If you fail, I will slit your throat." Little Sanchez learned that the only thing a woman was good for was to satisfy a man.

When he was twelve, Little Sanchez killed his first man.

Manuel and his wife Maria wandered the scrub country of West Texas following their small goat herd. They were barely able to scratch out a living among the scorpions and rattlesnakes. The rattlesnakes were always welcome. Their meat was tasty roasted over a fire. The couple had recently decided that this nomadic life had become too harsh. Manuel placed his gnarled hand over Maria's. "I think this would be a good time to go back to Mexico. Maybe some of our family is still alive. We have survived on the flesh and milk of our goats, but they are not as many as they once were."

Tears formed in Maria's eyes. "I have dreamed to go back to Mexico. Could we go today?"

Manuel smiled as he nodded.

Sanchez and the Comancheros watched the scrawny herd of goats from atop a mesquite ridge. They were being driven south by an old man and an old woman. Sanchez remarked, "If I had to live like that, I would kill myself." Sanchez slapped his leg as he quirted his horse into a short lope. He laughed. "Vamanos, muchachos! We must help the old ones."

Manuel and Maria backed away as the Comancheros rode through their goats. As the goats scattered, the bandits began shooting them. Manuel shouted, "Stop! Do not hurt my little ones!"

Sanchez replied, "But, señor, we were planning a great feast. Your goats are the guests of honor." Sanchez snickered at his own joke.

The Comancheros began butchering the goats. Sanchez ordered, "Dig a pit. We will feast on cabrito." Manuel and Maria had been forced to their knees.

One of the outlaws asked their leader, "What should we do with them?"

Sanchez responded, "Kill them… Wait, don't touch them." Sanchez motioned to Little Sanchez. "Come here, chico. There is more that you need to learn." Sanchez cocked his pistol and handed it, butt first, to the boy. "You kill them."

Little Sanchez hesitated. He had seen torture and death almost every day since coming to the Comancheros, but he was still only twelve. Sanchez screamed, "Did you not hear what I said! I said kill them or I will kill you!" The boy pointed the gun at the head of Manuel. He steeled himself to pull the trigger. At the blast from the gun, Manuel's head shattered. Red blood and gray brain jelly splattered on Maria. She sobbed in terror.

The murder of the old man caused the Comancheros to shout and cheer, "Little Sanchez is now one of us!" Sanchez proudly smiled at his adopted son. Little Sanchez had wondered before what it would be like to kill a man, but he didn't have any idea the impact it would have on him. To his surprise, he felt an exhilaration of joy. Little Sanchez also reveled in the approval of the gang. He laughed as he recocked the gun. The men joined in his laughter as he poked the old woman with the muzzle of the pistol. Little Sanchez discovered that day that not only did he enjoy killing, but he equally enjoyed watching the suffering of others. When he tired of the torture, he triggered another shot. Maria's blood and brains mingled with that of her husband's. Her body fell across Manuel's.

The Comancheros ate and drank all within sight of the two bloody corpses. It actually reinforced their feeling of power. No one or nothing could stop them. Little Sanchez drank himself into a satisfied stupor. Sanchez was more deferential toward Little Sanchez as time went on, but the bandit was still contemptuous of the boy.

Sanchez ruled the Comancheros with an iron fist. He did and said things his way because he could. It was irritating to Sanchez that there was a tiny flicker of fear in his heart. He didn't like the look that started to show in Little Sanchez's eyes. Sanchez thought, *I don't like what I am now seeing. Surely the chico would not try to challenge me. If he does, I will crush the hijo de puta!*

A year later the situation boiled over. Sanchez shouted, "Chico, I have told you many times that I will divide the money we get as I see fit. I know you have taken some of the money from the robbery of that cowboy. I know you found him and killed him. That is not important. All money goes to me. I will share it if I want! It is not up to you." Sanchez pistol-whipped Little Sanchez, leaving him bloodied and unconscious.

Sanchez made a mistake. He did not think that Little Sanchez would use the gun that Sanchez had given him against the outlaw leader. Sanchez passed out that night in his usual state of drunkenness. Drool dribbled from the corner of his mouth. A half-filled bottle of tequila slowly dripped on Sanchez's chest. Sanchez didn't hear the pistol cock. He didn't even feel the first bullet puncture his heart. The rest of the Comancheros were awaken by the gun blast. Most of them flinched with every shot as Little Sanchez emptied the six-shooter. The only reaction from Sanchez was a slight stiffening of his body as the slugs slammed home.

All the bandits had a weapon pointed at Little Sanchez. The boy never acknowledged them as he continued to stare at the object of his hatred. Finally, one of the Comancheros holstered his pistol. He spat in Sanchez's direction, "Good… I never like that hijo de puta! He did not give me my fair share!" No one made a move to bury Sanchez. Thunder Cloud assumed control of the band. He immediately started to divvy up Sanchez's possessions. All noticed that he gave Little Sanchez an equal share. A few muttered that Little Sanchez was just a boy. They were silenced by a disapproving look from Thunder Cloud.

That night as the gang sat around a campfire enjoying roasted stolen beef, Little Sanchez made an announcement. "I do not want to be called Little Sanchez any longer. My name is Sanchez!"

One of the Comancheros stated, "I thought we got rid of that sum bitch." Some started to smile. Then a raucous laughter exploded from the outlaws. It took a considerable time for the guffaws to die out.

Thunder Cloud was a little older than the rest of the Comancheros. While he was just as ruthless, he was a little calmer and more reasoning. The Comanche seemed like a logical choice to be the new leader. The Comancheros were a mix of half-Mexicans and half-Comanche. The band didn't divide itself along racial lines. They didn't care about that. The Comancheros were cutthroats, thieves and killers. Their concern was money, drinking, raping and killing. For the most part, the Comancheros maintained good relations with the Indian tribes. All the different tribes were considered trading partners.

The Federales in Mexico were also looked on as trading partners. That is until the presidency of Mexico changed hands. There was no election. The old president was shot by a military firing squad one day. The next day the army installed a new president. The new president was a figurehead. The country was really being run by General Felipe Ortiz. General Ortiz had a distaste for the Comancheros. He felt like whatever business was generated, it was too minor to hold his attention.

General Ortiz gave a command to his staff. "I want the Comancheros eliminated."

His captain responded, "Which band, General Ortiz? There are three separate ones."

The general barked, "All of them! Execute them all."

Thunder Cloud set up the raid on the small village of eighteen Pueblo Indians. They were diggers and farmers. The Pueblos were not known for their fierceness in battle.

Thunder Cloud commanded, "Kill the men, but do not harm the women. We will sell them to the Federales. They will use the women as whores to keep their army happy."

It was like shooting trout in a dried up mountain stream with only a single pool left. Thunder Cloud screamed his war cry, "Scalp the men!" The Pueblos fled in a panic. The Comancheros easily shot and stabbed the men. Thunder Cloud knew it would be dangerous to try to stop his men from raping the Indian women. He decided to let his men get their fill. Thunder Cloud hoped there would be enough left of the women to make them useful as whores. He told Sanchez, "Collect the hair. The Federales might pay for that." Sanchez did what Thunder Cloud wanted, but not before he took his turn with the women.

Thunder Cloud entered the little cantina in Juarez. Normally, Indians were not allowed in cantinas. This one was different because it was a point of contact between the Federales and the Comancheros. The Comanche downed a shot of mescal before telling the bartender, "Get word to the Federales that I have some business with them. We will meet them at the usual place."

The bartender asked suspiciously, "Where is Sanchez?"

Thunder Cloud tersely replied, "He is feeding the coyotes."

The only Comanchero who suspected anything was Sanchez. It was a feeling of dread that started in his belly and traveled up to the short hairs on his neck. The captain of the Federales sat on his horse in the middle of the clearing. Despite his young age, Sanchez had attended several of these trading sessions. It was usually scalps and women in exchange for gold. The young Comanchero thought it was curious that there were only two soldiers flanking the captain. Usually there was a full platoon. When the sun reflected off a rifle barrel in the surrounding trees, Sanchez wheeled his horse as he raked the animal's ribs with his spurs. He shouted, "It's a trap!" There was a volley of shots from the hidden soldiers.

Their Indian hostages were abandoned in the bandits' escape. Monetary gain took second place to survival. When the gang crossed the Rio Grande to the safety of Texas soil, Sanchez pulled up his pony to see if they were being followed. After watching for a few minutes, Sanchez exhaled. "It looks like them back-shooting Mexicans decided to take their time with the women." Sanchez wiped his brow with his sleeve as he surveyed the men. "They must have got Thunder Cloud."

The Comancheros rode for a couple more hours before stopping to eat. As they were eating, Rodriquez pointed out, "We got to come up with a new leader. I think I should be the one. Nobody knows more about being an outlaw than me."

After a brief pause, Sanchez responded, "I think it should be me. I'm the only one smart enough to figure out we were being bushwhacked."

Rodriquez retorted, "You? You're just a kid! You ain't been off your momma's teat for that long."

Without any warning, Sanchez pulled his pistol, shooting Rodriquez in the chest. The blast shocked the rest of the men. Sanchez calmly walked over to the dying bandit and put a second slug in his head. Sanchez seemed fascinated at the blood pooling under the body. Finally, he looked up with a smile. "Anybody else want to lead this pack? If you do, you can join this sum bitch." Most of the gang avoided his gaze. A few just grinned.

In the end the bandits had to admit the kid was smart enough to sniff out the ambush. One of them whispered to another, "Hell, if it don't work out, we'll drygulch the little son of a bitch."

There were always a few low-life drifters that Sanchez could add to the gang. The band was now twenty strong. Sanchez confided in no one. He kept his own council. The Comanchero chief was cunning enough to not trust thieves, killers and backshooters. Each man had proven that he would do anything if the price was right. Sanchez thought, *I need more men. I don't want to just be able to rob a stage or train. I want to take over Texas. Maybe one day I will be the governor of Texas. For that I will need an army.*

The next step in Sanchez's plan started to unfold. There was another gang of Comancheros in south Texas. This bunch was half the size of Sanchez's. Sanchez decided to combine the two groups. He sent out a couple of scouts to locate the smaller band. Soon the scouts returned with their location.

Sanchez stepped out in an opening next to the outlaw camp as the sun was starting to rise in the east. He proclaimed, "Who is the leader of your Comancheros?" The startled outlaws immediately became wide awake. It had never been necessary to post a guard. They were many miles from any kind of lawman.

A cocky man swaggered up to Sanchez. "I am Julio Torres. These are my Comancheros."

Sanchez held up and hand, curling his finger. As his gang appeared out of the shadows, Sanchez announced, "These are my Comancheros!"

Torres swallowed hard, "Very good. We must find some way to work together. To make everyone money."

Sanchez grinned. "I agree. We must be together!" Sanchez jerked his six-gun, firing a bullet into Torres' forehead. At the shot, the rest of Sanchez's bandits leveled their guns at the competing gang.

Sanchez stood over the body of the dead man. He admired the colors of his handiwork; the red blood, the white skull fragments and the gray of the jellied brain gore. Sanchez growled as he addressed the rival gang, "Here is your choice. You can join my band... No, make that my army. Or you can join Torres, feeding the worms!" Not surprisingly, all the old members of the Torres band became new members of the Sanchez Comancheros.

The Sanchez Army didn't bother to try to catch anybody by surprise. They rolled into the small West Texas town of New Boston. The Comancheros simply shot anyone seen on the two streets of the town. Sanchez entered the only saloon. He roared to the bartender, "Give my men all the whiskey and tequila they want!"

The bartender timidly asked, "Who's going to pay for all that?"

Sanchez cocked his gun, holding the muzzle an inch from the end of the nose of the bartender. He asked, "Is there a problem?"

The sweating bartender replied, "No, sir! No problem at all. I'll get right on it!"

Sanchez slapped the bartender so hard that it knocked him over, then he smirked. "Good man."

Sanchez stood on the wooden walk in front of the saloon. His men became silent waiting on orders from their leader. Sanchez stated, "Search every house. Bring any valuables to me. I also want the good people of New Boston tied up and also brought to me." Sanchez started back into the saloon. He shouted over his shoulder, "Get to work!"

The old woman tried to hide her necklace with her hands. She pleaded, "Please, no! That's all I've got to remember my mother by." The Comanchero jerked the necklace from her neck. She wept bitterly as she was dragged from her house.

The thirty-four men, women and children of New Boston were forced to kneel before Sanchez with their hands tied behind their backs. Sanchez preened in front of the assembly, his men and his captives. He proclaimed, "I am Sanchez! I am your new king! From now on I will be addressed as King Sanchez!" Insanity was fairly commonplace among the Comancheros. After all, to become a Comanchero, you had to be a Mexican or an Indian who didn't fit in well with their own culture. The stunned look on his men's faces said they weren't expecting this. The townsfolk were also in shock.

Sanchez cleared his throat. "Each of you will have a job. If you don't do your job, you will be shot. If you complain about your job, you will be shot. Whatever happens to you is up to me. The women's job is to please and take care of my men. You will do anything they ask of you. The men will do the work required to assist my army. You will take care of our horses and butcher the cattle to feed my men. You will also do whatever is asked of you. Refuse or complain and you will die!"

Sanchez walked through the captives pointing at every female above the age of ten. He commanded, "Take them to the hotel."

One of the captives who was a husband to one of the women and a father to a girl objected, "Now hold on there!"

Sanchez shot him between the eyes and raised an eyebrow. "Anybody else?"

One of Sanchez's men whined, "King Sanchez, there is an old woman who is useless. All she does is cry. Something about a damn necklace. It makes it very hard to use her."

Sanchez shrugged. "If she can't do her job, kill her. My laws are the same for everyone."

The bandit went back to the hotel. He tossed the naked woman on the bed. He cursed as he rolled off her. "Damn whore! You can't say I didn't give you a chance!" He slung the old woman through the back door of the hotel. The killer fanned his pistol, pumping three bullets into her. He snorted as he spit on her carcass, "You was warned!"

Sanchez summoned two of his most reliable men. Although he didn't trust anyone, Sanchez knew they would always do what was in their own self-interest. That made them easy to manipulate. Jose bowed at the waist. "Yes, King Sanchez." Chaytan likewise bowed, "Yes, great chief."

Sanchez threw up his hands in disgust. "Dammit, Chaytan, how many times I got to tell you I ain't no chief! I'm a king! Damn Indian!" Chaytan wasn't the brightest of men. It never registered to him what Sanchez actually wanted.

Jose looked on expectedly. Sanchez continued, "Jose, I can't get it out of my head about that small band of Shoshone up at the Wind River. I suspect they might have some women we can add to our hotel bunch. These women are wearing out pretty quick. They just don't make women like they used to. Take this halfwit, Chaytan and a dozen of our men. Bring me back some Indian gals."

On their way north, the raiding party discovered the Crow village. Jose gave a brief thought to attacking them but discarded that because there were too many Crow. While they spied on the Indians, Chaytan kicked his horse into a trot towards the Crow camp. Jose said in a loud whisper, "Chaytan, get back here!" When Chaytan didn't respond, Jose muttered, "Damn fool Indian!" Jose watched with trepidation.

What Jose did not know was that Chaytan was half-Crow. Chaytan rode into the village with a hand raised in greeting. "I am Chaytan! My mother was Quiet Rose!" Jose was certain that Chaytan would be filled with arrows. Instead, he was greeted warmly. Chaytan dismounted, sitting around the campfire. He asked the chief, "I am with a war party. We want to make war on the Shoshone. Where is their village?" Jose sighed with impatience as Chaytan appeared to be in no hurry. After eating and smoking, Chaytan jumped on his pony and returned to the Comancheros.

After several minutes of giving a hard stare to Chaytan with no response, Jose asked in disgust, "Well… What was that all about?"

Chaytan smiled, "Those were my people."

Jose continued, "Anything else? You were down there a long time. And why didn't you invite me to join you?"

Chaytan gave a slight shrug. "The Crow hate Mexicans."

Jose closed his eyes, slowly shaking his head. As Jose led the Comancheros away, Chaytan called out from the rear, "I know where the Shoshone village is."

Jose wheeled his pony around, "What?"

Chaytan responded, "My Crow brothers told me the last location of the Shoshone village. Even if they've moved, they should be easy to find. The Crow no longer live in the mountains because of a demon that protects the Shoshone."

Jose smirked in disbelief. "Indians!"

The Shoshone had not moved, choosing to rebuild the village on the original site. But this time, guards were always posted by orders of Chief Jack Flint. Jack spent less time running traps. He felt he was needed more with the Shoshone. Indeed, the Indians looked to the great warrior for advice.

Jack laughed as he watched Kit Bear frolic in the sunshine. Kit Bear was not old enough to walk, but his crawl made him mobile enough to get into mischief. Kit had left that morning to run traps. It was a way of life with the old mountain man. Trapping was in his blood. Jack enjoyed running trap lines, but not like Kit did.

Jose and the Comancheros silently observed the peaceful scene from a grove of aspens on a far ridge. Jose muttered as he counted, "There are six women. King Sanchez will be pleased when we bring them to him. There is one that may not go to the hotel. She is so beautiful that the king may keep her for himself. The rest of them, we will kill." Jose decided to wait for the cover of darkness before attacking. He anticipated that the surprise to the Shoshone would be so great that resistance would be minimal.

The hair on the back of Jack's neck began to rise. That always seemed to happen when there was unseen danger. As night fell, the Shoshone appeared to retire to their teepees. Jose didn't consider it odd that no nightly campfire was built.

The Comancheros rode as close to the village as they could. There were no guards. Jose's cries for blood split the calm of the night. The rest of the Comancheros joined in screaming war whoops and threats. They galloped unimpeded into the center of the camp. The marauders were welcomed by a volley of shots from rifles sticking out of teepee flaps. Six of the Comanchero saddles were emptied. Jack sprang from his teepee leaping on the back of a killer's horse. He slashed the Comanchero's throat before jumping to the next pony. As he felt the sting of the blade, Chaytan shrieked, "It is the demon! It is the demon!" Chaytan was thrown to the ground where blood gurgled from his throat.

Three other bandits were killed by the thumping of arrows into their bodies. Only two Comancheros remained. Jack dispensed with one by dragging him from his horse and driving his knife into the outlaw's temple. When it went in to the hilt, Jack gave it a twist for good measure.

Jack jerked the last attacker from his pony, pinning him on the ground. He held his knife at the Comancheros throat. He tried to escape, but Jack was just too strong. Jack demanded, "Who sent you? You are going to die. Your answer determines if it's a quick death or a slow one. Being skinned alive is very painful."

Jose replied, "We were sent by King Sanchez."

Jack was confused. "Who the hell is King Sanchez? There are no kings in this country!"

Jose started to choke as the point of Jack's knife started to sink into the soft flesh, "You will find out who King Sanchez is when he comes to look for us. He won't be coming alone. He will bring his army!" Jack ended the conversation by thrusting his blade into Jose's throat.

Jack didn't want to drag the bodies off where they might attract wolves and bears. He also didn't want to desecrate the crevice where the Shoshone were buried. Jack decided to pile the bodies together and burn them. When all that was left were skulls and bones, the Shoshone ground them up into a dust. They scattered the remains of the Comancheros. There wasn't enough there to show that the band of killers even existed.

A couple of days later, Kit came back from running his traps. The smell of smoke was still in the air. When he noticed the remains of the fire, Kit exclaimed, "Dammit, it looks like I missed quite a feast. Is there anything left?"

Jack grinned. "Nope!"

Kit studied Jack's face. "All right, out with it, boy. I can see something is bothering you."

It took a minute for Jack to respond. "One of the Comancheros babbled something about that some king and his army would come look for him. He knew I was about to kill him. Why would a man lie at a time like that?"

Kit replied, "Who knows why men say the things they say? He might have had too much whiskey. Besides, them

Comancheros are as crazy as a goat on loco weed. I say don't lose no sleep over it."

Jack responded, "Maybe…"

In a couple of days, Jack told Mountain Mist, "I need to protect our people. I would be a pretty sorry chief if I didn't. One of those Comancheros threatened us before he died. My gut tells me the threat is real. I am going to go see for sure if it's real. I'm don't know how long I will be gone."

Mountain Mist replied, "I trust you like I trusted my father to do what is best for our people. Kit Bear and I will be waiting on your return."

Jack pulled Kit to the side. "I can't shake thinking about that king nonsense. I'm leaving in the morning to find out if there's any truth in it. I need you to watch over Mountain Mist and Kit Bear for me."

Kit groused, "Dammit, Jack. You used to not leave me behind. Now, you're always traipsing off somewhere without me."

Jack smiled at his friend. "Before, I didn't have a wife and baby. You're the only one I can trust to keep them safe."

Kit watched Kit Bear crawling around, then answered, "Dammit it all to hell! You know I can't refuse when that boy is involved!"

Jack smile broadened. "Thanks!"

It was a relative easy task to back track the Comanchero raiding party. Jack circled wide of the Crow village, picking the trail back up farther south. Jack observed New Boston at a distance. He noticed the armed guards manning the entrances and exits to the town. Jack watched the guards refuse admittance, turning away anyone who didn't meet their approval.

The first night Jack slipped into town at about midnight. He had stripped down to a loin cloth. Jack carried his bow, arrows and skinning knife. He crouched under the window of the cantina. Jack heard Sanchez say, "Where in the hell is Jose and the rest of my boys? They should have been back by now. If that sum bitch has gone into business for himself, I'll skin all of them!" As Jack peeked in the window, he saw a Comanchero approach Sanchez. The man bowed at the waist. "King Sanchez, we did as you commanded. What would you have us do tomorrow?" Jack could not understand the muffled response. He was stunned to learn that there was a king. Jack had seen earlier that the king had enough men for an army.

Jack decided that he needed to take Sanchez's focus off the band that had not returned. He also knew that the odds against him should be whittled down. When the sun came up the next morning, shouts and screams were heard all over town. Ten of the Mexican Comancheros were found dead. Some had arrows in their hearts. The others had their throats slit. All were scalped.

Sanchez was livid. "Find whoever did this! I want him begging on his knees!" A search party was quickly formed. They weren't gone long before they returned to the cantina.

One bandit reported, "I'm sorry, King Sanchez. We could find nothing. There were no tracks."

A suspicious Sanchez retorted, "It must be someone in town. I want all the Indians locked up."

The Mexican Comancheros were given a secret briefing regarding the jailing of the Indians. They surprised their fellow gang members with drawn guns. The Indians were outraged. As the cell doors clanged shut, several shouted, "You will be sorry you did this!"

Sanchez oversaw the arrests. He responded, "It's your own fault, you scalpin' sum bitches! This is what happens to them that goes agin me."

Sanchez was at ease that night. He patted himself on the back. "I took good care of that problem. Ain't been no king who ever lived that was better at being a king than me." Unfortunately for the king, the Angel of Death in the form of Jack Flint paid another visit to New Boston.

The Comanchero gasped as his head was locked in a vise-like grip from behind. He tried to struggle, but he could not stop the blade from gashing his throat. The dying Comanchero could only feel the blood gushing down his shirt from the knife wound. When his eyes rolled back in his head, Jack silently laid the body down. Jack then sliced off a sizeable amount of hair. This scene repeated itself nine more times. Jack wanted the number of victims to match the previous night's total. He wanted the king to know that the assassinations were planned and not random. Jack knew that would create maximum panic.

The Comanchero rushed into the cantina the next morning. He had such a sense of horror that he did not bow. The bandit blurted out, "King Sanchez, there have been more killings. Their throats have been cut and they were all scalped, just like before!"

Sanchez jumped up from his table. "That is not possible! Are there any Indians not in jail? Did we miss someone?"

Sanchez summoned what was left of his gang together. There were about a dozen still alive. He commanded, "I want everyone looking for this murderer! Forget any other duties! Find this bastard!"

A frustrated band of outlaws returned to the cantina. One reported, "We found nothing. No tracks. Nothing!"

A bewildered Sanchez finally said, "We need reinforcements. Turn the Indians loose. Tell them I want to see them."

When released, the Indians did not go see their king. Instead, they followed the plan they had decided on last night. They mounted their ponies and rode out of town. Most of them didn't like having a chief, much less a king.

When the reinforcements didn't show up, the icy hand of fear began to squeeze Sanchez's heart. He flinched at the slightest noise. Jack grinned as he watched the deserting Indians ride off. He thought the time had come for a more direct confrontation with Sanchez without the cover of darkness.

The Comancheros went back to guarding the main road leading in and out of town. Sanchez hoped that would prevent the killer from coming back in. The two guards on the west side of New Boston weren't sure what to do next. One whispered to the other, "Maybe them Indians had the right idea. Maybe we should vamanos." The second outlaw's response was a gagging sound. The first one snapped his head around. He witnessed the terrifying cause of the gagging. His partner had an arrow stuck through his neck. The Comanchero clutched at his throat as blood began to trickle from both sides of the arrow. The first bandit screamed, turning to run. Another arrow thudded in the middle of his back. The point was sticking out of his chest. He fingered the point in disbelief before slumping to join his amigo on the ground.

Jack silently eliminated the rest of the Comancheros, one by one. Finally, there was only one left. Sanchez startled when Jack, clad only in a loin cloth, suddenly appeared before him. Sanchez demanded, "Who are you? Why are you not bowing? Do you not know who I am?"

Jack snorted. "I know who you are. I also know what you are."

Sanchez sputtered as he reached for his pistol. "You will regret this, señor!"

Jack was too fast. He jerked Sanchez's gun away from him. Jack laid the barrel of the gun across the bandit king's head, knocking him unconscious.

Sanchez awoke shrieking in pain. He was staked out in the middle of the street while his skin was being peeled from his naked body. Every citizen could hear the screams, but no one rushed to Sanchez's aid. Most smiled at the scourge of New Boston being brought to justice. The killing and rape of the good folks of the town was being avenged.

The tantalizing smell of roasted elk was savored by Jack as he approached home. Kit had killed a nice tender weanling that morning. The Shoshone embraced the feast. Mountain Mist was the first one to see Jack. She shouted, "Jack!" as she rushed to him. The entire village immediate began trilling a welcome to their chief.

After he dismounted, Jack embraced and kissed his wife. He was reminded how much he missed her. Jack's eyes widened in surprise as Kid Bear lurched towards him. Jack exclaimed, "When did he start walking? He's too young to walk!"

Kit chimed in, "That's why you had the good sense to name the boy after me. I do things ain't nobody done yet. He's just taking after his Uncle Kit. Next thing you know, he'll be running his own trapline."

Around the communal campfire that night, Jack related his trip as he smoked. He nodded his head between puffs. "There was a king and there was an army. The king appointed himself as king. He ruled from fear because the people hated him. Sanchez was responsible for many thefts, killings and rapes. He would have eventually been a threat to the Shoshone. Sanchez and his men no longer live." Most of the Shoshone understood that their chief was the one who ended the threat.

That night under the bearskin robes, Mountain Mist whispered in her husband's ear, "I am ready for another child."

Jack grimaced, "Damn woman, you sure know how to put pressure on a man."

Mountain Mist laughed. "I already know you can handle it."

Jack grinned. "I guess I better do my duty."

After a couple of weeks, Jack decided to put out a new trapline. Kit exclaimed, "It's about time you quit all that gallivantin' and get back to work. I'm not sure that them traps of yours ain't rusted shut." Jack thought he would try out a little valley he hadn't trapped before. He knew there were streams that should hold beaver.

While exploring the new grounds, Jack sucked in his breath at what he saw. It was a grizzly track. A huge grizzly track. Jack gave a low whistle. "Now that just can't be! It ain't possible." Jack cut his eyes around searching the trees. He looked back down at the track. Surely there couldn't be two grizzlies the size of Slew Foot. Jack said to himself, "But I saw him die. I know he was dead." Dread took root in Jack. Slew Foot was alive and he was back.

When Jack shot Slew Foot, the ball didn't penetrate the bear's thick skull. It lodged on its surface. The sting of the bullet soon went away. When Slew Foot drifted around the bend of the river, a sudden cough expelled water from its lungs. The massive grizzly paddled then waded to the shore of the river. He lay exhausted for several hours before reviving and wandering to find food.

Jack told Kit in a guarded voice, "It's back. I thought it was dead. Now I ain't so sure."

Kit frowned, "What's back? You gotta give me more to go on than that. What are you talking about?"

Jack lowered his voice some more. "Slew Foot. I think the sum bitch is back."

Kit retorted, "What?"

Jack motioned for Kit to lower his voice. "Keep it down, dammit."

Kit responded, "What makes you so all-fired sure it's back? Besides, didn't you shoot that bastard?"

Jack nodded. "I shot him all right. He just won't stay dead. Have you ever seen another grizzly with that size track? I'm telling you, it's him."

After arguing with himself whether he should or not, Jack told the tribe about his suspicions. Jack called the Shoshone together. "I have some bad news. I thought I had killed Slew Foot. It looks like I was wrong. Somehow, he survived. I saw his track in a small valley about ten miles from here. I'm sure it was him." A collective gasp of horror went up from the Indians. Nothing had ever inspired the sheer terror in them like the giant bear.

The huge grizzly ripped out the steaming guts from the elk calf. The calf bleated briefly before dying. When Slew Foot had devoured the remains of the elk including flesh, hide and bones, he was still hungry. The bear's ears pricked up when he heard the far off nicker of a horse. His eyes narrowed and his tongue licked his chops as he headed in the direction of the sound.

Lou Gleber had trapped the Wind River Range for several years. His efforts to make a go of the farm he had inherited from his pa turned into a disaster after his father's death. Lou was born and raised on the small plot of land in Mississippi. His mother had died giving birth to Lou. Two years of drought was the death knell for the farm. Lou packed up everything he could salvage, moving west to what he hoped was a land of promise.

When he stopped in Fort Smith, Arkansas, an old man sitting in a cane-back chair on the porch of the mercantile offered a piece of advice. Between spits of tobacco, the old man asked, "Where you headed, young feller?"

After scratching his head, Lou sheepishly admitted, "I don't reckon I rightly know. I know it's somewhere I don't have to be a dirt farmer."

The old man laughed. "I never cared much for farming myself. If I was younger and still had my strength, I know what I would do. I would head to the mountains and be a trapper. Yep, that would be a man's life."

Lou learned a lot of hard lessons during his first year in the Wyoming mountains. He almost starved to death being educated in the ways of a mountain man. Lou had a packhorse he had raised from a colt. He named the horse after his pa, Abel. Lou knew that Abel was someone good from the Bible.

Abel began prancing and snorting. Lou pulled on the lead rope. "Abel, what in the world is the matter with you? I hope you ain't having one of your contrary spells. Me and you are gonna have a problem if you start that."

Lou's blood ran cold when he heard a set of large jaws snap shut. He knew immediately it was a bear. Lou was torn between running or trying to save Abel. Lou didn't get a chance to think long. The grizzly charge was overwhelming. Abel was almost decapitated with one swipe of a massive paw. Slew Foot pounced on the back of the fleeing mountain man. Despite his sheer bulk, the bear had incredible speed. Slew Foot ripped off one of Lou's arms with his first bite. The bear lifted his bloody muzzle and roared in delight. He alternated between sinking his teeth in horse flesh and human flesh.

Jack confided in Kit, "If Slew Foot is back, I've got to find him and kill him."

Kit shook his head. "Boy, you get some of the craziest ideas. Why would you want to do something as fool as that? Do you just want to be bear shit?"

Jack laughed. "I've imagined myself to be several things, but bear shit isn't one of them. Look, if it was just me that would be one thing. But I got people counting on me... I can't just can't wait around until that bear decides to eat one of my family or one of the Shoshone. I have no choice. I'm going after him."

Kit sighed wearily. "I guess that means you want me to hang around and be a nursemaid?"

Jack replied, "I can't go hunting this bear and worry about my family at the same time."

Kit walked off muttering, "I wonder where exactly did I lose my balls? I used to have a pair."

When Jack told Mountain Mist what he was going to do, she froze. "No Jack! That is not a regular bear. It is an evil spirit. You can't go!"

Jack hugged his wife. "I have to go. Slew Foot is in our territory. It's just a matter of time before it finds us. I'd rather I find him than he find me. I have no choice."

Mountain Mist tightened her grip on her husband. "Please be careful. I will be praying to the Great Spirit to protect you. Kit Bear and I need you."

There were several offers from the Shoshone warriors to go with him on the hunt for the great bear. Jack responded, "It is best I go alone. If I took every brave in the village, we could not stand against Slew Foot. I need to kill him before he knows I'm there." The Shoshone nodded in understanding.

Some say a bear cannot remember an individual man. Slew Foot remembered Jack. He recalled what he looked like. The grizzly knew how Jack smelled. Slew Foot hated men, but he had a special hatred for Jack because of the pain the man inflicted on him.

Jack went to the last place he saw the grizzly's track in the small valley he had hoped to trap. Predators are different from prey. The prey animals are always ready to flee. They will only fight when cornered. A predator is mostly unafraid. Slew Foot was at the top of the predators. He had no fear of anyone or anything. Because he had no fear, Slew Foot was easy to track. The grizzly never gave a thought that something would try to find him and kill him. Any living thing was prey to the giant bear including other bears.

Jack trailed the giant grizzly to the massacre of Lou Gleber. The ground and the surrounding tree trunks were splashed red with blood. There was a couple of partial horse hooves and a tiny piece of a leather saddle bag. The bag had the initials 'LG' stamped on it. Jack recognized that it belonged to Lou. Jack shook his head as he muttered, "I ain't never seen anything like this." He was amazed that the forest floor and some of the trees were shredded. During his blood lust, Slew Foot attacked anything he could reach with his sharp teeth and massive claws. The grizzly seemed bent on destroying everything in his murderous rage regardless whether it was alive or dead.

Jack was already cautious. Now he crept along a few inches at a time. Jack paused motionless as he looked and listened. He had left his horse back at the village preferring to create as small a presence and scent cone as possible. Jack stuck to the edges of thickets. He realized if Slew Foot saw him before he saw Slew Foot, he would probably be killed.

The bear seemed to meander with no destination in mind. During the second time tracking Slew Foot, Jack was curious why the grizzly began traveling in a straight line. After a few hours, a horrible feeling came over Jack. He realized Slew Foot was headed to the village. Jack abandoned his wariness as he ran in pursuit of the killing machine. A vision of Mountain Mist and Kit Bear in those monstrous jaws caused Jack to run even faster.

As he neared the village, Jack heard the thunderous roar of Slew Foot followed by a rifle shot. A sick feeling rose up in Jack's belly. When he sprinted into the Shoshone camp, Jack saw the bodies of several of the warriors who he knew and loved. Jack's breath caught in his throat when he saw the huge grizzly standing on his hind legs as he advanced on his prey. Slew Foot was clicking his teeth together as saliva dripped from his fangs. Kit was standing in front of Mountain Mist who was clutching Kit Bear to her breast. The rifle shot had been Kit's. The old mountain man brandished his skinning knife as his only defense left against the marauding bear.

Jack dropped to one knee, sighted his rifle and put a ball in the back of Slew Foot's skull. The grizzly didn't seem to notice. Jack jerked his knife from its scabbard as he climbed its back from behind. He began stabbing the bear and screaming, "Come for me, damn you! Leave my family alone!" Jack held little hope that he could kill Slew Foot in hand-to-hand combat. He just wanted to distract him enough where his wife and child might get away. The sting of Jack's knife irritated the grizzly. Slew Foot shook his body in an attempt to dislodge the man. In the meantime, Jack had its neck in an iron grip. The Shoshone chief rapidly thrust his blade into the bear's throat.

Kit grabbed Mountain Mist by the arm as he ordered, "Run while you have a chance! Save the baby! I will stay and help Jack!" Kit charged the grizzly with a raised knife. Slew Foot never felt Kit's blade. A slight flick of its paw knocked Kit unconscious.

Slew Foot started to roll to get Jack off its back. Jack stubbornly kept his grip and continued to stab the bear. The loss of blood from its many wounds began to take its toll on the grizzly. Its fur became slick with blood, making it harder to hold on. Jack felt a slight wobble from Slew Foot. He kept stabbing its throat. The grizzly began to crumple, but it was a long way from dead. Even at half strength, the bear was still incredibly powerful. When much of the starch was gone from Slew Foot, Jack reloaded his rifle. He nestled the muzzle of the gun between the grizzly's eyes. The blast from the rifle partially exploded Slew Foot's skull. The bear continued to thrash around. Jack muttered, "Die, you sum bitch, die!"

After one last shudder, Slew Foot died, taking his legacy of death and destruction with him. Kit sat up, groggily asking, "What happened?" He quickly regained his focus. Kit leapt to his feet when he saw Jack standing over the massive body of the grizzly. Kit shouted, "Is he dead? Is he dead?" Jack's response was to collapse to a seated position. Kit ran to him, "Boy, is you all right? Are you hurt?" His friend was drenched in blood. Kit didn't know whose it was, Jack's or the bear's.

Jack grinned up at Kit. "I think I'm all right. I ain't certain yet. I'm wore out."

When Mountain Mist saw the grizzly was dead, she rushed out of the thicket where she was hiding. She carried

Kit Bear as she ran. Mountain Mist had tears flowing down her cheeks. She exclaimed, "Jack! Are you hurt?"

Jack chuckled as he slowly regained his feet. "I don't think so. I haven't completely checked yet, but I think I still have all my body parts. I'm just tired."

Mountain Mist embraced her husband then fetched a deerskin rag for Jack to wipe his face and hands with. Jack grabbed Kit, hugging him tightly.

The old mountain man protested, "Boy, have you taken leave of your senses? Dammit, let me go!"

Jack pushed Kit to arm's length. Tears welled up in Jack's eyes. "I saw what you did. You were prepared to die defending Mountain Mist and Kit Bear."

An embarrassed Kit responded, "Well… hell… I just figured I was too old to ever get another kid named after me." Jack hugged Kit again. Kit shouted as he tried to pull Jack's arms down, "Now dammit! There you go again! Stop it, boy, or I might just let the next bear et you!"

Jack and the rest of the village sadly buried the three dead warriors in the deep crevice. It took three days to skin Slew Foot and start drying its meat. The pelt made six robes. There was a profound satisfaction among the surviving Shoshone that the curse that was Slew Foot was no longer a part of their lives.

Meanwhile, in a secluded mountain den many miles away, a large silvertip female grizzly curled up for the hibernation. She could already feel the life stirring in her belly.

Before Jack jerked Snake Eye from the land of the living as he did to his father, Scar, Snake Eye fathered a son. This baby was the product of a rape just like his father before him. His mother was glad when she heard of Snake Eye's death. She remembered how horribly Snake Eye hurt her during the rape. In fact, the whole tribe of Crow were also glad about Snake Eye's death. They also rejoiced at the killing of Scar.

The baby's mother, Gentle Breeze, prayed that her child would be nothing like his father. She named the boy Sunrise, hoping he would brighten her day. At first Sunrise was just like the rest of the Crow children. There were some bickering and minor skirmishes like most children engage in. Certainly nothing that one of the women couldn't sort out.

At three years of age, Sunrise began separating himself with his behavior from the other children. There was a cruelty about Sunrise that was different from the others. When going hunting with the older boys, any rabbit or squirrel that was arrowed but wasn't dead was tortured by Sunrise. He laughed at the squeals from the rabbit or squirrel when Sunrise tried to pull off an arm or leg while the animal was still living.

Finally, one of the older boys cuffed Sunrise on the side of his head, commanding him, "Stop that! You're not showing the proper respect for an animal that gave its life that we might live."

Sunrise's eyes narrowed, "If ever you do that again, you will be sorry!"

The older boy was twice the size of Sunrise. Still, that didn't stop a shiver from going up his spine when he gazed into Sunrise's eyes. Even though the bigger boy laughed at

Sunrise's threat, that didn't prevent a queasy feeling from boiling in his stomach.

Over the next few years, whispers started around the village. "I think Sunrise is infected with the same evil spirit of his father and grandfather. He has a bad heart." Some will say that insanity cannot be inherited. While that may be true, there was no denying the cruelty shared by Scar, Snake Eye and now Sunrise.

Gentle Breeze did everything she could to bring out a good spirit in her son. Encouragement and scolding netted the same results—a stony stare from Sunrise. The current chief of the Crow, Kenesaw, tried to provide guidance and wisdom to Sunrise. The chief counseled, "Little One, every man in life must find the path of a true man. Your father and grandfather rejected the good path. They chose an evil one. You have the same choice. Choose wisely."

The six-year-old boy snorted in derision. "I will go my own way!"

Kenesaw was not used to being treated in such a disrespectful manner. He considered banishing Sunrise from the tribe, but he did not take that action because of Gentle Breeze. She had suffered much. He did not want to add to her pain.

Kit Bear was now seven years old. He was growing up straight and strong. Jack beamed whenever he saw Kit Bear. He said to Mountain Mist, "Every father should be proud of his son. My pride in Kit Bear goes past the normal pride. He is strong, fleet of foot, but has a compassion for others. There are those that say he will succeed me one day as chief. I think that he would be a good choice."

Mountain Mist smiled. "He grows more like you every day."

Kit overheard their conversation. "Well, maybe he's a little like his pa, but I think he really takes after his Uncle Kit."

Jack and Mountain Mist laughed together.

One day, Kit Bear had planned on going hunting with his best friend, Wild Wolf. Whenever Jack was not available, Kit Bear was with Wild Wolf. They were constantly testing each other. Wild Wolf smirked, "Have you forgotten that I beat you in the last foot race?"

Kit Bear retorted, "I'm not sure you beat me! No one was there to judge. If I hadn't tripped over that tree root, it wouldn't have been close."

Wild Wolf replied, "Ha! You always make up some kind of excuse when I'm better than you."

Kit Bear grinned. "Make up some excuse? I don't need excuses to beat you."

The give and take dissolved into a playful wrestling match. When they were exhausted, Kit Bear said, "Are we going hunting are not?" Both boys jumped up, grabbed their bows and headed into the woods.

The gray wolf was gaunt. You could count his ribs through his hide. The wolf had developed an abscess in a tooth, making his whole mouth sore. It was difficult for him to chew. The wolf was slowly starving to death. It watched the young boys creeping through the woods, searching for game. Normally a wolf would not attack a man, but this one was desperately hungry. It warily observed the boys from his concealment in a dense grove of trees. Driven by an overpowering need to eat, the wolf began to stalk the young Shoshone.

Wild Wolf whispered, "Where are the elk and deer?"

Kit Bear whispered back, "If you don't shut up, we'll never see anything."

Both boys froze when they heard the guttural growl behind them. The wolf charged. Even though both bows had arrows nocked, there was no time to use them. The wolf was heading for Wild Wolf. Kit Bear dove between them, slapping at the predator with his bow. The wolf's jaws closed over the arm of Kit Bear. In his weakened condition, the wolf could not bite as hard as he normally could. Wild Wolf thrust his arrow by hand into the wolf. He drew out his knife, stabbing the wolf repeatedly. Despite one arm being mangled by the predator, Kit Bear managed to get out his knife, plunging it repeatedly into the attacker. As the wolf drifted toward the land of the dead, Kit Bear felt the pressure on his arm lessen. When Wild Wolf saw the wolf was dead, he gently pried its jaws off his friend's arm.

Kit Bear was bleeding profusely. On their way back to the village, he stumbled and fell as he lost consciousness. Wild Wolf gathered him in his arms, running back to the Shoshone camp. Jack saw them coming and rushed to meet them. He took Kit Bear from Wild Wolf. Wild Wolf gasped for air. "He saved my life! Kit Bear saved my life!"

Jack hurriedly carried his son to his teepee where a concerned Mountain Mist began treating him for his wounds. She murmured, "You will be all right, son."

After Jack could see that Kit Bear was going to be live, he stepped out of the teepee. Wild Wolf was sitting there waiting. He exclaimed, "I am sorry, my chief!"

Jack replied, "There is nothing to be sorry about."

Wild Wolf stated again, "Kit Bear saved my life!"

Jack rested his hand on the young Shoshone's shoulder. "I think y'all are even because you saved his as well."

Wild Wolf was relieved that the people would not fault him for Kit Bear's wounds.

The flap to the teepee was thrown open. Kit burst in. He roared at Kit Bear even though it was apparent that the boy was resting comfortably, "I heared you done tangled with a wolf! Tell me where this varmint's at! I'll hunt the sum bitch down and skin him alive!"

Kit Bear laughed. "Thanks, Uncle Kit. I'm all right. Besides, me and Wild Wolf have already killed that varmint."

Kit started to simmer down. "Well… okay… But I wish you'da left him for me. I wouldn't have gone as easy on him as you boys probably did."

Kit Bear grinned. "I know, Uncle Kit. If you had gotten him, there wouldn't have been enough left of that wolf to wipe my ass."

Mountain Mist exclaimed, "Kit, see what you've done? Quit teaching my son that type of language!"

Kit responded meekly, "Yes, ma'am." When Mountain Mist turned her back, Kit gave Kit Bear a broad wink.

When Kit Bear was recovering, his friend visited him many times. Wild Wolf asked, "Why did you throw yourself in front of that wolf?"

Kit Bear grinned. "Because you needed help! I knew I was stronger and faster so it was up to me to save you."

Wild Wolf replied, "I needed help? I needed help? If it wasn't for me dragging you back to the village, you would be wolf shit right now!"

Mountain Mist smiled at things returning to normal.

The Crow nation became more and more concerned about Sunrise. Most of the parents forbade their children from playing with him. This was after a number of incidents when a child would be out of sight with Sunrise and come back injured and crying. When asked about what happened, Sunrise would shrug. "Your son is clumsy. He tripped and fell." Surprisingly the children would not say what really happened. Anyone could see that they were terrified of Sunrise.

After his son was hurt, one of the warriors approached Sunrise. Sunrise left his feet from the force of the blow. The Crow pointed his finger. "You might cause fear in our young ones, but I am not afraid of you! If you touch my son again, I will kill you!" Normally the other adults would object to another adult who was not the parent disciplining a child that harshly. None of the other Crow said a word. Even Gentle Breeze wasn't upset. She was concerned Sunrise was going to come to a bad end, but she didn't know what to do about it.

Honking Goose received encouragement from the other Crow for confronting Sunrise. He nodded. "Someone needed to do something." A week later, Honking Goose went out in the woods to relieve himself. As he squatted, he felt a sharp pain in his back. When Honking Goose twisted around, he saw Sunrise with a bloody knife. The Crow warrior gasped, "You!"

Sunrise gave an evil smile. "Yes, it's me. You should have known better than to hit me. Your son wouldn't have been that stupid."

As Honking Goose knelt in his own excrement, the boy plunged his knife into the man's throat. The warrior grasped his throat trying to stop the flow of blood to no avail. Honking Goose pitched forward. His face was covered in the manure. Sunrise laughed out loud at the sight. He vowed his enemies would all suffer the same fate.

An outcry rose from the Crow at the discovery of Honking Goose. Soon the entire tribe were trilling at the tragic news. The fact that the Crow warrior was found in his own excrement made it worse. No respectable Crow likes to be humiliated. Chief Kenesaw marched to Gentle Breeze's teepee. He ordered, "Sunrise, come out! Bring your knife!"

Gentle Breeze whispered to her son, "What have you done?"

Sunrise snickered. "Nothing! I have not done anything."

Kenesaw examined the knife. He announced to the watching Crow, "There is blood on this blade." The chief demanded, "Where did the blood come from, Sunrise?"

Sunrise smirked. "I killed a rabbit earlier. That's probably its blood."

Gentle Breeze came out with a rabbit carcass. Chief Kenesaw snorted, turning around as he stomped off. He knew Sunrise killed Honking Goose. The entire village knew who the murderer was. Sunrise was just too cunning to be caught.

When Sunrise was twelve, he made an announcement. "Chief Kenesaw, I challenge you for the right to be chief of the Crow!" A challenge by combat was a long-established tenet of the Crow, although the only time this right was invoked was when there was a bad chief.

Kenesaw laughed. "Sunrise, you are just a boy. I could easily kill you."

Sunrise shrugged. "Then kill me."

The warriors began to argue among themselves if one as young as Sunrise could challenge. Finally, the chief raised his hands for quiet. "Maybe this challenge would be a good thing to do. It might solve several problems."

Gentle Breeze knelt at the chief's feet. "Please, he is just a boy! He does not know what he's saying."

Kenesaw was unmoved. He thought about the murder of Honking Goose. He replied, "No, we will fight. Sunrise is old enough."

Kenesaw was a seasoned fighter. One of the reasons he was chief was due to his bravery and fierceness in battle. He never considered the possibility that Sunrise might win. A warrior tied their wrists together with a leather strap as was the custom. Each combatant was armed with a knife. Kenesaw was overconfident as he towered over the boy. The chief was planning on being merciful. One knife slash across

Sunrise's throat should end the combat and the challenge. The tribe could return to normal.

The Crow was not prepared for the speed of the boy. He moved like a rattlesnake strike, diving between the legs of Kenesaw. That pulled the chief a little off balance allowing a split second of time for Sunrise to drive his knife up into Kenesaw's groin. The pain caused the Crow chief to react with shock. Sunrise thrust a second, then a third time into his genitals. Blood began to flow in streams. Kenesaw's face turned white as he toppled over in death.

Sunrise cut the leather strap, leaping to his feet. He jerked the dead chief's hair and scalped him. Sunrise shouted as the held the bloody scalp for all to see, "I am Sunrise! Chief of the Crow! Any who oppose me will have their hair decorate my lodge pole!"

The people were stunned. Other than the shouting of Sunrise, there was silence from the Crow. Finally, someone muttered, "He has a demon." Fear quickly spread over the village. Sunrise was their new chief and they all feared him.

Towa and Zuni were Pueblo Indians living in caves on a sheer cliff in what is currently Colorado. The Pueblos were peace-loving, preferring to pull up their long ladders at night to protect themselves against the more war-like tribes. The women farmed. The men sometimes helped, but also hunted small game like rabbits and squirrels.

Towa remarked as he watched his children play in the sunshine, "Zuni, the lack of rain has hurt our crops. I will soon take some of the men on a hunting party. Rabbits have disappeared. We need larger game like deer and elk. Our village must have meat quickly or our old ones will die."

Zuni responded, "Please be careful! It always makes me nervous when you get too far away from our caves."

The women and children of the village gathered to send off their men. Only ten accompanied Towa. The rest stayed behind. Towa had spoken at the communal campfire, "I will take a few men hunting. We may be gone for a while. The rest of the men will stay to protect our women and children." Zuni sadly watched her husband ride away as the tribe trilled their goodbyes.

Towa shook his head in disbelief. "Where are the deer and elk? There are no rabbits either." The recent drought had been devastating to the wildlife. The hunting party pushed deeper into the mountains searching for game.

The young Crow warrior galloped his pony into camp. He slid off its rump before coming to a complete stop. The brave rushed up to Sunrise and breathlessly exclaimed, "My chief, it is a war party not far from here."

Sunrise raised both eyebrows. "What tribe would be foolish enough to challenge the Crow?" Sunrise dispatched one of the old warriors to confirm the report.

When the warrior returned, he had a big smile on his face. "It is not a war party. It is a band of Pueblos! They are farmers, digging in the ground like women! There are ten riders. None of them are warriors."

The young Crow who brought in the first report became embarrassed that he had misjudged the threat to the village. He ducked his head pulling back into the crowd.

The look on Sunrise's face was one of anger. It looked like a storm cloud ready to spit lightning. Sunrise shouted, "I don't care who they are! They have no right to be this close to our village. Prepare for war!" The entire camp began shrieking and screaming war whoops, demanding death to the Pueblos.

Towa heard the din from a long way away. At first, he was confused as to the source of the noise. As the shrieking came closer, Towa realized it was angry Indians. Towa kicked the ribs of his horse as he shouted to the other hunters, "Back to the village!" When the Crow closed the gap on the Pueblos, Sunrise was almost insane with blood lust, screeching and foaming at the mouth. He spooked even his own men.

The Pueblos were outnumbered three to one. The first two farmers were killed when a Crow leapt on the back of their pony. The Crow warriors savagely stabbed them in the back. Both Pueblos died while still on their horses' backs. When Sunrise saw how easily the Pueblos died, he shouted, "Do not kill them! I want them alive!" Eventually the eight surviving men were captured. Their hands were bound behind their backs. They were put on their horses and led to the Crow camp. Sunrise smiled at what he had in mind.

The Pueblos were humiliated that night around the Crow campfire. They were beaten with clubs by the Crow women and children as they screamed, "Dogs! How dare you claim you are men?" The Crow men thought it great sport to urinate on their hapless victims. One of the warriors patted another on the back. "Your aim is as good as it is with a bow." A woman squatted over one of the Pueblos, also urinating on him. This led to peals of laughter from all the Crow.

The next day Sunrise ordered, "Bury two of the dogs in holes with only their heads above ground. Slice off their eyelids. I want them to see all that will happen to them. Smear their heads with honey."

At their chief's request, one of the warriors dug up a red ant bed, dumping the fiery ants over the exposed heads. The Crow village laughed themselves into a state of exhaustion at the screams and pleadings from the tortured.

The following day, Sunrise pointed at two large posts in the middle of the camp. He declared, "Tie two more there." Firewood was stacked around the squirming men. The Pueblos began to cry in horror. They knew what was coming. There was something different about the smell of human flesh burning. Different from the charring of animal flesh. Sunrise threw back his head, taking a big breath of the sweet aroma. He observed to the Crow closest to him, "I love that smell!" The Crow nodded in agreement. All in the tribe were too intimidated of their leader to disagree with him.

Sunrise was irritated at how quickly the first four of his captives died. He preferred more suffering. The next two were staked out naked with their arms and legs secured. Sunrise slowly scraped his knife over the inner thigh of one of the Pueblos. The man cringed at the touch of the blade. Sunrise laughed, "Since you lived like a dog, you should die like a dog." Sunrise peeled off an inch of skin. The Pueblo howled in pain. Sunrise heated his knife in the fire before scorching the wound, effectively cauterizing it. He was able to keep the first man alive for three days before he died. The second man only lasted two. During the skinning process, the Crow Chief wouldn't allow anyone else to do the skinning. He enjoyed inflicting the pain too much.

The last two prisoners were hung upside down with their hands tied behind their backs. A deer carcass was butchered in the same manner. Towa was one of the men. He was in despair as he had watched his fellow tribesmen die horrible deaths.

Sunrise was in good spirits as he hacked of the genitalia of his victims. He smiled as he held up the meat, "See? Just like a deer!" Even the Crow gasped as his blade bit into the soft underbelly of Towa. The Pueblo's last thought was of his wife and his children playing in the sunshine. Sunrise proceeded to butcher the hapless captives. When Sunrise stacked the quartered men, he gestured to his people, "Eat!" To some of the Crow, cannibalism was revolting. They ate anyway out of fear of offending their chief. Others consumed the human flesh without a care.

White Antelope waited until his lifelong friend, Wahkan, was alone. The two Crow were the elder members of the tribe. White Antelope said in a soft voice, "Wahkan, I cannot take any more of this. Our chief has no respect for our people or our ways. I thought things were bad with Scar and Snake Eye. Together they don't match the little finger of Sunrise. We have to cut out this evil. I am prepared to die if it is needed."

Wahkan sighed, "I agree with you, my brother… but how? Neither of us have the strength anymore to kill Sunrise in combat. If you can think of a way, I am with you."

White Antelope replied, "I have given that some thought. We would not give a rattlesnake a chance to defend itself. We would kill it in a manner that would put us in the least amount of danger. We should do the same to this despoiler of our people."

White Antelope and Wahkan patiently waited until Sunrise went into the woods to relieve himself. With a slight nod from White Antelope, the two Crow launched arrows at Sunrise. The arrows struck the Crow chief in the shoulder and leg. Neither shots were fatal. Having been committed, the elders rushed Sunrise with war cries. White Antelope shouted, "Your time has come! You are finished as our Chief!" Wahkan screamed, "You must die! Our people will suffer no more!"

The look on Sunrise's face never changed. He calmly jerked out the arrows, laughing at the charging old men. Sunrise side stepped White Antelope. He thrust his knife into the belly of the elder Crow. White Antelope stumbled and coughed before falling over. Blood gathered in a pool under his body. Wahkan had tried to help his old friend but was too slow. When Wahkan reached out to catch the wounded White Antelope, Sunrise sliced his throat from ear to ear. White Antelope and Wahkan lay side by side in the dirt as their lifeblood drained from them. Wahkan managed to grasp White Antelope's hand before he died. They were friends in life. They were friends in death as well.

Most Crow were accustomed to pain and torture. What Sunrise did next went beyond the pale. After dragging the bodies of White Antelope and Wahkan into the center of the camp, Sunrise announced, "Let the oldest sons come claim the bodies of these traitors." When the two Crow stepped forward, Sunrise quickly slashed their throats. With a war cry, Sunrise thrust his bloody knife skyward, "Let it be known that Sunrise will not tolerate traitors among the people!"

Jack sat cross-legged by the campfire. He pensively gazed into the flickering flame. Jack thought back over his life. How he lost his white parents and became an Apache. How he lost his Apache parents and became a trapper, meeting Kit

Bridger who was his best friend. Now he was the chief of the Shoshone. Jack smiled at the thought of Mountain Mist and his son, Kit Bear.

Jack moved his hands closer to the fire for further warmth. He spoke softly to himself, "I only wish that I didn't have this knot in the pit of my stomach that the Crow was still going to be a problem and that Slew Foot wasn't dead. Hell, the Crow don't even live in the mountains anymore and I ate Slew Foot. It doesn't make any sense."

The chief of the Crow screamed, "The blood of my grandfather, Scar, and my father, Snake Eye, cry out for revenge! I, Sunrise, will not rest until the Shoshone are no more!"

The female grizzly gave birth, but the cub was so large that it killed her during delivery. The cub sucked what milk there was from her lifeless teat. When he had no choice, the cub gorged himself on his mother's flesh. He grew big enough to break out of the den.

The End

Printed in Great Britain
by Amazon